In the laidback Florida Keys, former spies Nick Seven and Felicia Hagens found a paradise far removed from the covert world of the CIA.

Nick, content to run a bar on the Gulf and maintain a low profile, breaks his self-imposed exile when a friend asks for help in getting a local mob boss off his back.

Popular singer Jimmie Rae wants to get free from the notorious Turk Morgan, a crooked music mogul who controls the Miami entertainment scene. Jimmie reveals that his girlfriend has gotten caught in Turk's web, and he wants to get her out before it's too late.

As Nick and Felicia explore the neon jungle of South Beach, they encounter the dark underside of the music business. Drugs, prostitution, street thugs, and political payoffs are Turk's stock in trade, and he isn't one to relinquish control over his empire.

Nick goes undercover as an international criminal to challenge him, but will he succeed in breaking Turk's hold over Jimmie and his girl? Can Nick use the sting operation to solve a cold case murder he discovers by accident? What other secrets will he uncover?

The Neon Jungle
Copyright © 2019 Tim Smith
ISBN: 978-1-4874-2554-8
Cover art by Martine Jardin

Published by eXtasy Books Inc or
Devine Destinies, an imprint of eXtasy Books Inc

Look for us online at:
www.eXtasybooks.com or www.devinedestinies.com

THE NEON JUNGLE
NICK SEVEN BOOK 6

BY

TIM SMITH

DEDICATION

For Randy Smith

CHAPTER ONE

October in Key Largo is called the slow season. Right after the dog days of summer and right before the cold northern climes bring the annual influx of snowbirds and timeshare dwellers. Many of the bars and restaurants on the island close and give their staff a two-week vacation. Nick Seven had never followed that pattern since he assumed ownership of Cricket's Bayside. It wasn't that he was greedy, just savvy enough to realize the locals still needed someplace to party, and it might as well be his club.

He sat at his private table on the outdoor deck, gazing at the multi-hued sunset over the Gulf. The palette slowly changed from bright blue to azure to yellow with a strong orange tint. Wisps of clouds leftover from an early afternoon rain added a dark contrast, silhouetting the boats in the distance. Along the fishing dock that extended over the inlet next to the club, a few seagulls and herons had staked out their favorite pilings, their keen eyes scanning the shallows near the sandbar for any stray fish careless enough to venture too close to shore.

A gentle evening breeze mussed his thick brown hair. Nick sipped his scotch on the rocks. Glancing over at Felicia Hagens, he took in her bronzed Barbadian complexion, long brown hair, and high cheekbones. His gaze traveled over her torso, lingering on her full bosom pressing against her light blue polo shirt.

Luckiest thing that happened to me after we both got out of the spy business was when Felicia came to live with me. She knew I'd never forgotten my late wife and the guilt I felt when she was killed in a terrorist attack meant for me, but that didn't stop her from carving out her own place in my soul. I should thank her for that.

In the last few years, he'd spent a helluva lot of time watching her, day after day, doing a thousand mundane little things to change his hermit-like existence. He had learned to appreciate the in-your-face honesty, the erotic ease they shared in bed, the quiet conversations under the stars with a glass of wine, a lingering touch on the cheek, and the gentle teasing accompanied by a sexy wink and smile. All of that in one beautiful, sensual package reminded him of the life he had shut himself off from.

She looked at him, and her face blossomed into a smile. "What're you starin' at?" she teased in her West Indies accent.

"I was just noticing how the sunset brings out the luster in your hair. In fact, in this light, you look like a sexier version of Halle Berry."

"In what picture?"

"*Die Another Day* but you definitely fill out a bikini better than she does."

Felicia raised her glass. "Can't argue with that." She sipped her Cuba Libra, looking at the setting sun. "It's so pretty and peaceful this time of day. Reminds me of home."

"Pretty sunsets on Barbados?"

"Mm-hmm." She looked into his eyes. "But not quite as nice 'cause I didn't have someone special to share them with."

Nick brought her hand to his mouth and kissed it. "Great minds think alike."

He scanned the crowded deck and outdoor bar. The interior restaurant was busy as well, and the wait staff hustled trays with appetizers and entrees to those who were dining *al fresco*. People were engaged in conversations while listening to a local musician named Jimmie Rae as he played a variety of songs on his guitar and sang favorites and requests. Jimmie, trim, black, with short-cropped hair and a mustache, was one of those musicians who had the rare ability to play anything the customers wanted to hear, in every genre.

"He really packs 'em in, doesn't he?" Felicia asked.

"Uh-huh. We're lucky we can get him once a week. He's a big draw down here."

Jimmie finished his song to strong applause and addressed the crowd. "Gonna take a short break, but before I do, I got to play somethin' for someone important." He lowered his voice. "Actually, it's for the boss man sittin' over there in the corner. If I didn't do this one, he'd fire me."

The crowd chuckled as Jimmie tuned his guitar, started his background accompaniment, then launched into *On Broadway*, perfectly channeling George Benson. The crowd clapped in rhythm as he effortlessly glided through the opening guitar licks.

Nick smiled as he listened. "Whatever I'm paying him, it's not enough."

Jimmie finished his set to a loud ovation and placed his guitar on the stand. He stepped off the small stage and was instantly greeted by a few patrons, shaking his hand and posing for selfies. He got a drink from the bar before making his way to Nick's table.

"You sound good tonight, man," Nick commented.

Jimmie sat. "Thanks. This crowd's always easy to please."

Nick looked aghast. "Not my clientele. They're very picky."

Jimmie laughed. "Right. Get enough beer and tequila into people down here and they'll applaud *Chopsticks*." He sipped his drink. "Can I talk to you 'bout somethin'?"

Nick nodded. "I knew it. You want a raise."

"Nah, it ain't that." He hesitated. "I got trouble, and I need your help."

"What kind of trouble?" Nick asked.

"You heard about that gig my agent lined up for me next

month in South Beach, didn't you?"

"Yeah. Two weeks at Coconuts during the annual Latin culture festival. Sounds like a great opportunity. What about it?"

"You might've heard that when I was a kid, I got jammed up in some serious shit. Drugs, petty theft, you name it. I wasn't doin' right."

"Yeah, I heard about that, but you cleaned up your act. Lots of kids make mistakes, and you've made a good career for yourself with your music."

Jimmie took a deep breath. "One of the mistakes you didn't hear about was who made that career possible."

Nick eyed him curiously. "Who?"

Jimmie looked at him. "Turk Morgan."

"The Sultan of South Beach? How did he get his hooks into you?"

"Turk was a big man, always helpin' the poor folks in Liberty City and Overtown. Guess I got suckered into his game without realizin' it. He knew I wanted to get into music, and when he booked bands into his clubs, he'd let me hang out with those guys. They gave me guitar lessons and helped me develop my style. That was pretty heady stuff for a star-struck kid, and I liked the attention. Before I knew it, he was usin' me to do favors for him."

"Like what?"

"Playin' lookout for his pushers, tellin' his go-betweens if there was anyone hangin' around who was out of place in the neighborhood, that kind of stuff. That's how he built his street network. He does you a favor, and he expects one in return. If you fall for it the first time, he keeps on doin' you favors, and you keep on owin' him one more. It never stops."

"Come on, Jimmie. I can't believe you were ever that much of a pushover, even when you were a starry-eyed teenager."

Jimmie looked at him for a moment. "That wasn't all he

used. Turk's a clever son of a bitch. He knew my family was strugglin'. He'd slip my mom some money to pay the rent and put food on the table. The message was pretty clear, even for a fifteen-year-old on the streets."

"Sounds like he attended the Vito Corleone school of management. Did Turk get you hooked on drugs?"

Jimmie paused. "Indirectly. Guys backstage, they'd share a joint with me between sets. Then, I got into the hard stuff." He looked Nick in the eye. "But I swear, I kicked the habit, and I've been clean for five years."

"I'm still waiting to hear about this problem you want help with."

Jimmie shook his head. "I shoulda known Turk wouldn't leave me alone. When I got this gig in Miami, he contacted me. Said if I dropped my agent and came to work for him, he wouldn't let it out about my past."

Nick tapped his cigarette ash into an ashtray. "So what?"

"What do you mean, so what?"

"So, he threatened to out you. You stepped in front of it and turned things around. Did Turk threaten your family?"

Jimmie shook his head. "Family's gone. Nobody left in Miami but me."

Nick puffed his cigarette, thinking there was more to this than Jimmie was admitting. "What's the real problem you need help with?"

Jimmie hesitated for a few moments. "There's a girl named Jalisa. I met her in rehab. We clicked, ya know, goin' through the big kick together. After we got straight, we moved in together." He smiled wistfully. "Some nights I knew she was on the edge, but I'd hold her real close and tell her it's all right, baby. We can get through this. Just hang onto me. She was one sweet lady."

"Was?"

"She moved out a few months ago, but we're still tight.

When Turk called me, he made a point of tellin' me how Jalisa was part of his stable, one of his hangers-on, ya know?" He shook his head. "I can't let her get dragged back into that life. She deserves better than that."

"Do you think she's back on drugs?"

Jimmie looked into his eyes. "No, but Turk made it clear it wouldn't take much to get her hooked again. *Once a junkie, always a junkie*, he said."

"Is that why you want her back, to make sure she stays clean?"

"That and I just want her back in my life."

"Not to be too personal, but why did she move out? Did you two have a fight?"

Jimmie shook his head. "I was makin' a lotta headway with my career. My agent was keepin' me busy, and I was gone a lot. I think Jalisa was a little jealous of it. She's always wanted to be a singer and figured it was now or never."

"How did she get hooked up with Turk Morgan?"

"She was singin' back-up for some two-bit hip-hopper. This guy couldn't make it past the cheap clubs, but she thought it was a steppin' stone. Turk caught the act one night and convinced her to come work for him, said he could get her into somethin' better."

"Did he?"

Jimmie shook his head. "Not yet."

"When did this happen?"

"About two months ago." He hesitated. "You know what else Turk's into besides drugs, don't you?"

Nick exhaled a billow of smoke. "If you mean escorts, yeah."

Jimmie smirked. "Man, you're bein' polite, callin' his girls escorts. That makes it sound like a movie fairy tale. He puts 'em to work on the streets. Some do outcall, some of 'em hustle tourists in the bars, including his clubs." He hesitated. "If they complain too loud, they end up workin' off their debt in the dives in Overtown and Liberty City."

"Working off their debt?"

"When he brings anyone into his inner circle, they sign a contract for his management services, and he pays 'em a stipend until they start makin' it back. He does the same thing with the musicians he signs, only he uses them to push his drugs."

Felicia and Nick exchanged glances. "I can see why you're worried," he said. "Has he ever tried to sign you before this?"

"Coupla times, but I always said no. I'm not gonna get mixed up with him again."

"I know he has more than one nightclub, but which one does he use as his base of operations?"

"His pride and joy is Bahama Joe's in South Beach, but if you're thinkin' about sendin' the cops in, forget it. Turk's a smart cat. He never lets any business go down in there." He hesitated. "Nick, this job could get me a lotta exposure. My agent talked with a record producer in LA. The guy heard a demo I made, and he's interested in signin' me."

"Do you think that's why Turk wants you to work for him?"

"I can't think of any other reason. None of the acts he represents have any kind of following outside of Florida."

Nick gave him an analytical gaze, trying to determine the real motivation behind Jimmie's request. "Which is more important to you—getting your big break or getting your girl back?"

Jimmie's eyes narrowed, and he gave Nick a hard look. "I want him to leave Jalisa alone, and I really want her back in my life."

Nick nodded. "I just needed to hear you say it. Do you have a picture?"

Jimmie took out his phone and scrolled to the photos. He

held it out for both of them to see. They looked at the young woman with long braided brown hair, caramel complexion, tasteful make-up and jewelry, and a come-hither smile.

"She's very pretty," Nick said. "Why do you think I can help you?"

"I heard about what you did before you took over this place."

Nick let a sigh escape. *Here we go again.* "Jimmie, I turned in my decoder ring and cyanide pills a long time ago. This sounds like more of a domestic thing between you two, and I'm not sure I should get involved."

"Come on, Nick. Turk's a bad guy, and he destroys a lotta lives. I'm just afraid if she hangs around him, she's gonna get herself in trouble. I can't let that happen."

Nick took a final puff, then ground out his cigarette. "You really care about her, don't you?"

Jimmie cast his gaze down and smiled sheepishly. "That transparent, huh?"

"I've been there." He sipped his scotch. "Let me think about it."

Jimmie went back to the stage to play his next set. Nick heard a sigh and looked over at Felicia, slowly shaking her head.

"What?" he asked.

"Hon, things have been peaceful around here. Why do you want to change that?"

"I said I'd think about it. What's wrong with thinking about doing a favor for a friend?"

Felicia paused. "Nothin', I guess, but if you stop thinkin' and decide to start doin', give me a heads up."

"Why? So you can go back home for a visit?"

"No, so I can try to talk you out of it."

They focused their attention on the stage. Jimmie had picked up his acoustic guitar and turned the stage lights down a few notches. He sat on a stool, wordlessly launching into the classic gal-that-got-away lament, *Here's That Rainy Day*. The crowd became quiet, the good time chatter of before replaced with near silence. Jimmie didn't utter the lyrics, letting his nimble fingers glide over the guitar strings to tell the tale of worn-out wishes and leftover dreams. The longer he played, building to the climactic crescendo, the more emotion he poured into each chord. When he quietly finished, his eyes cast down, the crowd sat in stunned silence for a moment before bursting into a spontaneous roar of applause and whistles.

Felicia tightly squeezed Nick's hand, and the trace of a tear formed in the corner of her eye.

He wiped away the tear. "He really got to you with that one, didn't he?"

She glanced down. "Okay, so I'm a sucker for a happy ending."

"So am I. Do you want to help Jimmie get his girl back?"

Felicia gave a sheepish grin. "Why not? Things have been too quiet lately. You can start by tellin' me about this Turk Morgan guy."

Nick took a drink. "Turk Morgan started as a DJ on a Miami radio station, playing Funk, Hip-Hop, you know, the stuff the kids listen to. He was popular but apparently, it wasn't enough for him. He used his celebrity status to bring some name bands to Miami and organized music festivals. After his name and reputation got around, he signed a syndication deal and moved his show to satellite radio. He bought a few nightclubs and got into the talent management business."

"Bookin' bands doesn't sound criminal."

"Not until you add the natural by-products that seem to follow a lot of pop music acts."

"You mean drugs?"

"Along with booze, women, and payola. Turk became a master of the game. He'd book an act into a club, then strongarm the owners for a healthy chunk of the gate."

"How did he manage that?"

"You heard what Jimmie said about his network of street enforcers. He made his bones in the poorer areas of Miami, spread his money around, and surrounded himself with a lot of thugs. To make himself look respectable, he claimed to be a born-again Christian and aligned himself with a few religious leaders."

"His born-again persona is just an act?"

"A lot of people thought so. He used it to bring some high-profile names into the fold, like politicians, movie stars, and professional athletes. He even set up a couple of charitable foundations that give help to the poor, but he probably uses it to launder his dirty money."

"If he's into drugs and prostitution, why haven't the cops put him out of business?"

"No direct link between him and his alleged criminal activities. Too many buffers in place. He also greases a lot of palms and contributes to the right political candidates. He probably uses other methods, too, like blackmail and extortion."

"He ever set up shop down here in the Keys?"

Nick shook his head. "He's too smart for that. He knows if he ever sets foot in Monroe County, my very good friend, the sheriff, would run his ass out of town."

"How do you know so much about this guy and his network?"

"That's the interesting thing about owning a place like this. We get a lot of cops in here, and they love to tell war stories. I just listen."

She giggled. "You gonna talk to this fat cat and tell him to lay off Jimmie and his girl?"

"Guys like Turk Morgan don't exactly respond to please and thank you. I know I can't buy him off or scare him off. We'll have to figure another angle."

Felicia thought for a moment. "Sounds like he needs to be convinced it'd be in his best interest to let go."

Nick stared into the night sky while unlocking the inner vault of his memory. He took something from the shelf of the long ago and faraway and blew the dust off it. "Do you remember an operation we did in the old days where we convinced a weapons trader in England to find another line of work?"

"Yeah. We pulled a scam on him. Made him think his people bailed on him and set him up as the fall guy with his customers."

"That might work with Turk."

"You went undercover on that op, didn't you?"

"Yeah, as Nick Stavros, gunrunner for hire." He chuckled and slowly shook his head. "Haven't thought about that in a long time."

"Might be time to bring him out of retirement. What do we do first?"

"Talk to Jimmie's agent to get the full story, then check out the competition on South Beach."

She flashed a playful smile. "You're actually treating me to a night on the town?"

"Looks that way."

"And me without a thing to wear."

Nick's gaze scanned her torso. "You'd look good in a beach towel."

CHAPTER TWO

Nick and Felicia entered the office of Brillstein Talent As-sociates in mid-town Miami the following afternoon and looked around the nicely appointed waiting room. The walls were adorned with a few tropical motif paintings, mixed in with headshots of entertainers. Nick recognized a few of them. There was no secretary on duty, but Nick found an in-tercom next to an office door, with a security camera mounted above. He pressed the button and was greeted with a raspy "Yeah? Who is it?"

"Nick Seven. I called you earlier about Jimmie Rae."

"Hold your ID up to the camera."

Nick took his driver's license from his wallet and held it close to the lens. A moment later an electronic lock on the door clicked. Nick and Felicia looked at each other as they went inside.

Sid Brillstein sat behind his desk, which was littered with stacks of papers. He was in his shirtsleeves, rolled up to his elbows, and his paisley tie was loosened. He sported a deep tan and a hawk nose, and curly hair turning to more salt than pepper.

He gave Nick a penetrating head to toe steely look before he relaxed, stood up halfway, and stretched his hand over the desk. "Sorry, but I can't be too careful. You own Cricket's Bay-side in Key Largo, right?"

"That's right. This is my significant other and partner, Fe-licia Hagens."

"A pleasure. What can I do for you?"

They took seats. "Jimmie told me about the trouble he's having with Turk Morgan. I thought we might help."

Brillstein smirked. "Got an army?"

"No, just a lot of experience with these kinds of things. Tell me what's been happening."

Brillstein looked down for a few moments. "Jimmie's a big talent. I saw it the first time I caught his act. He could do better than these pissy little local clubs." He looked at Nick. "No offense."

"None taken. Continue."

"I called in a favor from a record producer friend in LA. Sent him a demo, whet his appetite, got him scheduled to come out here next month when Jimmie's booked into Coconuts. That's when I get a call from Turk Morgan, telling me he wants Jimmie to come work for him."

"What did you say?"

"I told him to piss off." He looked at Felicia. "No offense."

"That's okay," Felicia said while glancing at Nick. "I've heard worse."

Nick gave her a sideways glance while addressing Brillstein. "Go on."

"The next day a couple of his gorillas pay me a visit and tell me I should seriously reconsider the offer and tell Jimmie it would be in his best interest to play along."

"Or else?" Nick asked.

"I can tell you've been around. They didn't threaten me per se, but the implication was clear."

"Do you really think Turk would resort to physical violence to make his point?" Felicia asked.

Brillstein opened his desk drawer and withdrew a picture he handed across the desk. "Look at her."

Nick and Felicia eyed the eight-by-ten glamour shot of an attractive young woman, hair elegantly coiffed, make-up per-

fect to accent her bronzed skin, with tasteful dangling ear-
rings that complemented her glittery cocktail dress.

"Very pretty," Felicia commented. "Who is she?"

"You mean who *was* she," Brillstein corrected. "Her stage
name was Jasmine Blake. I caught her doing a karaoke night
at some dive in Homestead. I pegged her as an up-and-comer
right away."

He paused to fire up a cigar. Pointing his finger and speaking with more animation, he told them, "This girl had a voice
that could massage a set of lyrics like nobody since Natalie
Cole, and it wasn't only that. She had stage presence and
charm. Thirty seconds into a song, she could've coaxed the
crowd into following her into the Everglades."

"What did you do with her?" Felicia urged.

"I started her off slow," Brillstein said. "Got her a dynamite
accompanist, booked her into a few high-end hotel lounges, a
couple of conventions, then some smaller clubs out of town.
She was ready to move up. Hell, I was negotiating for her to
open for Sheryl Crow next year."

Nick's eyelids lowered. *Why do I think this story doesn't have
a happy ending?* "And then?"

Brillstein stared at him. "And then, Turk Morgan enters the
scene. Caught her act one night and decided she should be
working for him. He tried his usual soft-sell routine, but she
turned him down. He called me to convince her to take his
offer, but I told him I wouldn't do it."

"Did you bother to ask Jasmine how she felt about it?"

Brillstein puffed his cigar. "I ran it past her. She said no.
She knew who Turk was, and she didn't want anything to do
with him. She also liked how I was handling her career. When
I passed it along, he made his point the hard way." Brillstein
closed his eyes for a moment before he continued in a subdued tone. "Jasmine was finishing a club date, and when she
left, someone tossed acid in her face. Suffice to say, she never

sang in public again."

Nick and Felicia exchanged uneasy glances. "I'm sorry to hear that," Nick said.

Brillstein slowly wagged his head. "Not as sorry as I was for Jasmine. Bright, talented, beautiful young woman who could've had the world, but Turk Morgan took it all away."

"You're sure he was behind it?" Nick asked.

Brillstein stared at him for a moment. "The day after the attack I was at the hospital with her when I got a call on my cell phone. It wasn't Turk, but the guy told me that next time I get a serious offer, I should pay attention. Need I say more?"

"How does he work his hostile takeovers?" Nick asked.

Brillstein puffed his cigar. "He waits until I've put a lot of time and sweat into grooming someone until they're ready for launch. He makes contact, wines and dines them, drops a few expensive gifts and convinces them they could do better with him. All they have to do is sign away their lives and drop me like a boiled egg."

"That approach didn't work with Jasmine Blake?" Felicia asked.

Brillstein looked at her. "She's a smart young woman, and she knew how the game was played. Jasmine wasn't one of those reality show winners who expected to have a career handed to her. She was willing to work for it."

"There's something I don't understand," Nick said. "If you have them under contract, why not hold them to it or threaten to sue for breach if they leave you?"

Brillstein cast his gaze down for a few moments. "I tried that with the first one he stole from me. A couple of days later, I was getting into my car after work and one of his musclemen accosted me. He smacked me around and said if I stood in the way, I could expect worse, and so could my family."

"What did you do?"

Brillstein looked at him. "What the hell do you think I did?

I caved. The next day I got a certified check for five thousand dollars and a signed release from my former client."

Nick nodded. "That makes it look perfectly legal, a simple business transaction. Why not take that approach with Jasmine?"

Brillstein paused for a few moments. "In retrospect, considering what happened to her, I should have, but it was her decision, and I respected her feelings. She wanted to stick with me, and I was ready to put everything behind her to get her the career she worked for. Now he's trying to pull the same shit with Jimmie Rae."

"How many clients have you lost to him?"

"Ten, all headliners with a good local following. He also cost me a lot of business contacts. Turk put out the word and suddenly, I'm poison. Hell, there are club owners I've done business with for years, but he put the squeeze on them. I used to have the top talent agency in southern Florida. Now, if I offered them the second coming of Elvis, they wouldn't book through me."

"Have any of your former clients seen their careers skyrocket since they signed with Turk?"

"Not so you'd know it. They can't leave him, either. He locks them in with a personal services contract that keeps them indentured to him for ten years. The language in those contracts is so convoluted, it would take a legal scholar to find a loophole."

"Why does he let you stay in business?" Felicia quizzed. "If he's that intent on havin' everyone in his corner, why not just take all of your clients?"

"Because he's a sadist with a good press agent," Brillstein replied. "If he takes away my livelihood, to the public it looks like he's a heartless bastard. If he lets me earn a living, he's just a shrewd businessman. He also gets a good laugh at my expense."

"Why do you think Turk's taking a sudden interest in Jimmie Rae?" Nick asked.

"Aside from his popularity, the only thing that comes to mind is this recording deal. All of his other acts have a local following, but none of them can make it on the road. He probably thinks if Jimmie scores big, he can ride his coattails."

Nick thought for a moment. "When did you ink this deal and get your record producer friend involved?"

"Three months ago."

"When did Turk call you about buying out Jimmie's contract?"

"About a week later. Why?"

"Just curious. What's really important to Turk?"

"You mean besides the obvious?" Brillstein retorted before puffing his cigar. "His latest scam is opening a museum dedicated to Funk music. He wants to make it like that Rock 'n Roll place in Cleveland."

"I remember reading about that," Nick said. "He announced that project a few years ago, didn't he?"

"Yeah. He's been collecting donations ever since, but he hasn't broken ground yet."

"Where does he use the entertainers he stole from you?"

"Mostly in his clubs around town, and he loans them out to his competitors for a huge fee."

Nick's gaze shifted to the window, watching the traffic on the crowded street below. He thought for a moment as an idea came to him. "What does your partner have to say about this?"

"I don't have a partner."

"Wrong," Nick countered. "You have a silent partner named Nick Stavros. He's a gunrunner and smuggler from Queens, New York. He was busted from the army when he was caught selling weapons on the black market, and he's currently wanted by Interpol. He went underground twelve years ago and operates in Europe and the Far East. Now he's back in the States, and he isn't happy about someone poaching on his business interest."

Brillstein slowly rocked his chair, puffed his cigar, and pointed it at Nick. "You're Stavros. Right?"

"You catch on quick. Are there any of your former clients you still keep in touch with?"

He took another headshot from his desk and handed it over. "When bookings are slim, this one calls me to arrange something under the table."

Nick and Felicia looked at the photo of an attractive Asian woman with shoulder-length bright red hair, intricately painted nails, and a sly smile.

"Who is she?" Nick asked.

"You mean who is he," Brillstein corrected. "A drag queen who goes by the name China Peters. He's a big draw at some of the clubs. Really does well in Key West during Fantasy Fest."

Nick examined the photo a little closer. *Damn, talk about good make-up.* "I can see why. Are you still tight with her? I mean, him?"

Brillstein shrugged. "Yeah, I guess."

"Tight enough to get him to do you a favor?"

"Such as?"

Nick handed him the photo. "I need you to get word to Turk through the grapevine that your silent partner isn't happy about what he's doing. Make it sound like I'm a trigger-happy thug with a short fuse and a lot of juice. I've come to Miami to settle accounts. Can you do that?"

Brillstein eyed him warily. "What's this going to cost me?"

"Maybe a few restless nights until we take Turk down. Are you up for it?"

Brillstein chuckled. "I don't have a concealed carry permit for nothing. I can take care of myself and my family."

Nick handed him a business card. "My private number and e-mail are on that card. I'll need you to send me a list of all the clients he stole from you. Call me if you hear anything interesting."

He and Felicia stood and were about to leave when Brillstein stopped them, asking, "Why are you doing this?"

Nick looked at him for a moment. "I don't like bullies." He flashed a wink and a smile. "Keep in touch."

"You think he'll play along?" Felicia asked while they waited for the elevator.

"I think he'll do what it takes to get Turk out of the picture."

They entered the empty elevator, and Nick pressed the ground floor button. They rode in silence for a moment.

"What did you mean back there, when you referred to me as your partner?" Felicia asked.

"What do you think I meant?"

"I know the textbook definition of partner, and I know what it meant when we worked for the CIA."

"Your point is . . ."

"In which context were you usin' it?"

Nick looked into her soft brown eyes. "Partner, *i.e.*, one who plays on the same team as another."

"What team are we playin' on?"

He pulled her in for a kiss. "The team of life. Does that satisfy you?"

She giggled. "Yeah. You know somethin'?"

"What?"'

She rested her palm on his chest. "I like kissin' in elevators."

"You're such a thrill seeker."

Ocean Drive in South Beach was a steady parade of expensive sports cars and stretch limos. Every art deco-themed club along the street had people streaming in and out, accompanied by a blend of musical styles. Bright multi-colored lights washed over the stucco buildings and tall palm trees towered above the clubs and hotels, their waxy fronds reflecting the setting sun like a coating of gold dust. Lummus Park and the white sandy public beach were occupied by couples enjoying the early twilight and people taking a swim in the warm ocean. Pelicans and seagulls pecked at the strands of seaweed that had washed ashore.

Nick and Felicia sat outside a coffee bistro across the street from Bahama Joe's, taking in the colorful vista. The crowd was primarily young and dressed in the trendiest attire as dictated by self-appointed fashion mavens on some reality TV show. Nick looked at the old-style buildings, built during the halcyon money-laden days of old Florida. Rich northerners had flocked to Miami Beach for three months each and every winter, dropping piles of cash in their wake. It seemed there was always something new to replace a landmark drenched in history yet ignored by the current caretakers. More of the gorgeous mansions and hotels that made up the South Beach legacy suffered from the malaise of neglect. Thanks to the flashy vendors, the pulsing around-the-clock clubs, and the endless supply of hustlers and takers, the strip still held a powerful allure.

This place draws people in like a twelve-car pile-up on I-95. You know you shouldn't stop and gawk, but somehow you can't help yourself.

Nick puffed his cigarette and focused his gaze on Bahama Joe's while taking an occasional sip from a cup of coffee. The flashing blue and yellow neon sign above the front entrance spelled out the club's name in sexy, curvy letters and depicted a caricature of a man and woman in tropical attire locked in an embrace while performing a native dance.

Felicia took a drink from a bottle of mango flavored water. "It's gotta be eighty degrees out here. How can you drink coffee when it's this hot?"

"It's how I beat the heat. Keeps my internal thermostat high."

"It's also how you get dehydrated."

Nick continued watching the club. A black Lincoln town car pulled to a stop in front. The doors opened and three men got out. Nick focused the camera of his cell phone and zoomed in to take pictures of each man.

"The eagle has landed," he said.

"Which one is Turk?"

"The one in the middle."

Turk entered the club, flanked by a bodyguard on each side. His driver proceeded to the parking lot next to the club, nosed the car into a reserved space, and went inside.

"Let me see who we're up against," Felicia said.

Nick scrolled to Turk's picture. Turk Morgan was just over six feet tall, with a husky build and a shiny black bald head. He had gray mutton chop sideburns and a bushy gray mustache. He brought to mind a bulldog stuffed into an expensive tailored suit, a very angry bulldog.

"Looks kinda rough," she commented.

"I'm sure he is. Do you see where his car's parked?"

"Yeah."

He took a small GPS tracker from his pocket and handed it to her. "Put that where they won't find it."

Felicia crossed the street and fell in step behind a group of women walking toward the clubs. When she reached the parking lot, she splintered off but kept her head down, avoiding the security cameras while looking for something in her purse. Nick watched her remove a set of keys she dropped on the ground behind Turk's car. She squatted to pick them up, stood, and crossed the street.

"Nice work," he commented.

"We goin' in?"

"Not this time. I don't want our faces on the security cameras before we pay a visit."

"What about that tracker I put under his car?"

"It might help to know where Turk lives and where he goes."

"Hon, I know Jimmie's a friend and you'd like to help him out, but why do you really wanna get involved in this?"

He took a final puff, then extinguished his cigarette. "I keep thinking about the singer Brillstein told us about, the one Turk went after. I didn't make the connection until after we left his office, but she did a one-night stand at Cricket's a couple of years ago. She was a fill-in for someone who had to cancel at the last minute."

"You knew her?"

"Only to say hi to, but I remember she was pretty good." He looked at her. "I just can't fathom anyone doing something like that because they were told no. Makes me wonder what else Turk's into."

Felicia nodded. "Yeah, that struck a chord with me, too. What're you thinkin'?"

"I'm thinking this might be more than a two-person job."

"Why?"

"Did you see how much muscle he has surrounding him? I'm sure he has more working inside."

"I think we can handle it."

Nick tossed the empty coffee cup into a nearby trash receptacle. "Ask yourself a question. Would an international criminal who's wanted by Interpol risk going out in public without a bodyguard?"

"You could say I'm your back-up."

Nick looked at her. "No offense, but I have something else planned for you."

"Like what?"

"You're the diversion, the thing that gets Turk's body-guard to take his eyes off of the prize."

"And his mind off of his job?"

"No, nothing like that."

"Nick, I can handle myself."

"I know you can, but I don't want Turk to know, at least not right away. Let him think you're my arm candy, a demure pussycat."

Felicia chuckled. "I like the way this is goin'." She paused. "Who are you gonna get for the bodyguard role?"

Nick hesitated for a few moments, knowing that Felicia wouldn't like his answer. He responded in a low voice. "My former partner, Bones McCoy."

She groaned loudly, defiantly shaking her head. "No way. You can't trust him. Every time we get involved with him, somethin' goes wrong. Find someone else."

"Come on, Felicia. We need him on this."

"Why?"

"Several reasons. One, he runs a high-tech security company with resources and manpower we don't have. If we're going undercover, we'll need help establishing a phony background. Two, we'll need to run checks on Turk's people, especially any cops he has on his payroll."

"And three?"

Nick paused again. "I already called him."

"Without tellin' me first?"

"Because I knew you'd react this way."

She exhaled in exasperation. "Hon, I thought we had an understanding about things like this."

"We do, and I should've run it past you before I did it."

Felicia gave him a suspicious gaze. "We've been together since we left that agent's office. When did you call him?"

Nick hesitated. "After dinner, when you went to the ladies'

room." He shrugged. "Sorry."

Felicia was silent for a few moments. "What's the plan?"

"Hopefully Turk will hear about me through the pipeline, and he'll get one of his cop buddies to run a check to find out if I am who I say I am. While that's going on, we keep track of him for a few days to get his schedule down and dig into his operation. When we have some leverage, we'll visit him."

"You think he'll let loose his hold on Jimmie, just like that?"

"No, but I want him to think I'm a serious threat. That's why we aren't going in there until we get some ammunition. What do you think?"

"I like it." She paused. "Except for usin' McCoy."

CHAPTER THREE

Felicia sat at the computer in Nick's den the next morning, doing searches for Turk Morgan. She found numerous articles in the archives of The Miami Herald, all extolling his virtues as a humanitarian and philanthropist.

I guess if you've got enough money, it can cover up enough dirt. If people only knew.

Her mind drifted to the last few encounters they'd had with Nick's former CIA partner, Bones McCoy. While Felicia had to admit his help had been valuable and they had achieved the desired results, there was always the unexpected twist of the knife in the back.

Every time he's helped us, there was some personal motive, usually involvin' money or somethin' he could use to his own advantage later. I know he and Nick go back a long way, and they saved each other's hides a few times, but I hope he isn't blinded by that.

Nick came in with two cups of coffee. He set one on the desk and looked over Felicia's shoulder.

"Interesting," he commented. "Turk's an ordained minister? Who knew?"

"Couldn't tell it by what we know." She sipped her coffee. "When's McCoy gettin' here?"

"Any time now. Is this gonna be a problem?"

Felicia looked up at him. "Not as long as you lay down the ground rules and make sure he follows them."

"What ground rules?"

"There's no money in this caper and nothin' he can gain from it."

"I'll cover that. Anything else?"

She hesitated. "Just keep him off my back."

He rested his hand on her shoulder. "You have my word. Anything from the tracker you planted on Turk's car?"

Felicia switched to a different screen. "Visits to a club in Bal Harbor, an office building on Indianola Avenue, and a residence in Boca Raton. The car's been there since late last night. Probably where he lives."

"Boca Raton," Nick echoed. "You know what that translates to from Spanish to English?"

"Uh-huh. Rat's mouth."

Nick sat in a cushioned wicker chair, drinking some coffee. "I talked with Jimmie. He gave me some info about Turk's network. There's a cop on the Miami Beach vice squad named Vargas. Turk pays him a weekly stipend to look the other way and run interference when needed."

"We'll have to get around this dirty cop."

"That's one of the reasons I called in McCoy. If there's dirt on someone, he can find it. He also clued me in on Turk's main bodyguard, a badass named Salazar."

"How bad?"

"Jimmie said he likes to hurt people for fun and profit." He took a sip. "How's my fake background coming along?"

Felicia picked up a sheet of paper. "See how this sounds. Nicholas Stavros, age 42. Born in Queens, New York to Greek immigrant parents. Enlisted in the army after high school but was dishonorably discharged when they discovered he was sellin' weapons on the black market. Before they could bring him to trial, he fled to Europe and branched out into smuggling. He counted the IRA and the Russian mafia among his best customers. Went underground twelve years ago and hasn't been seen or heard from since." She looked at him. "What do you think?"

"Not bad. That should convince Turk that I'm a serious

threat. What have you found out about his empire?"

She pulled up a different screen. "He owns five nightclubs, a music promotion business, a radio station, and he's on the board of directors for two local non-profits. He has a charitable foundation that gives a helping hand to those in need, including food pantries, a soup kitchen, and a thrift store. They're all located in Overtown and Liberty City. There are a few other businesses listed, too. He's also the founder of a church and five years ago, some political action group tried to get him to run for state representative, but he turned it down."

"No surprise there, since his criminal enterprises would've been discovered."

"He probably figured he can't make any real money in politics."

Nick laughed. "Spoken like a true naturalized citizen. Wait until you've been in this country full time for a few more years and see if you still believe that."

She lightly smacked his arm. "Quit. I know the score." She continued reading. "No criminal record, but citations and awards from every organization you've never heard of."

"Anything about his finances or net worth?"

"Nothin' I could find. Everything he owns is privately held."

"What did you find out about his background?"

"He grew up in Liberty City, both parents deceased, no siblings. His official bio makes him out to be a hometown success story. You know, clawin' his way up from the gutter to the big time."

"What was that remark Brillstein made about him having a good press agent? You can dress up anyone in expensive threads to make them look respectable."

"I looked up his home turf. Liberty City is a lower to middle-income community for blue-collar types, most of them immigrants. If Turk's a local guy who made good, why doesn't he keep his base in his hometown to show support?"

"Money and fame have strange effects on people. He probably does most of his charity work there to make it look like he hasn't forgotten his roots."

She turned to face him. "But Boca Raton's the high-end part of Miami. From what I've read about him and where he conducts business, I can't see him livin' there."

"Neither can I. That's the stiff upper lip crowd. Lots of old money and dot-com millionaires who got out before the bubble burst. Not really Turk's kind of people. He must have a big bankroll if they let him live there."

"What do you mean, let him live there? That would be discrimination if they kept him out."

Nick drank some coffee. "You're right, but I do know one thing."

"What?"

"*I'm* barely white enough to live in Boca Raton."

Nick left to answer the doorbell. Felicia followed and saw Bones McCoy enter. He and Nick exchanged friendly greetings, a handshake and slaps on the back.

Never understood this whole bromance thing. Maybe I should watch more Dr. Phil.

She gave McCoy a cool, wary gaze. Tall and muscular, he had adopted the Florida look of a white linen jacket over an open-necked bright yellow silk shirt and tan chinos. His close-cropped beard and bald black head were offset by a gold spike in his left earlobe. He approached and extended his hand which Felicia reluctantly shook.

"Good to see you again, girl," he gushed. "You're lookin' good."

She gave a polite smile to hide her unease. "Back at ya."

They took seats in the living room. McCoy opened a manila envelope, removed some items and handed Nick two laminated cards. "Your new fake ID and concealed carry permit,"

McCoy said.

Nick examined the driver's license. "Looks real enough, but what about this address you listed? If Turk's got a cop on his payroll, he'll check this out."

"Got it covered. That's a condo my company leases. We use it for out of town customers. As of this mornin', your name's on the lease."

He handed him another item. "A credit card in your new name, linked to one of my corporate accounts with a twenty-grand limit. Just keep receipts. My accountant is funny that way. I also had our fraud department put a red flag next to your undercover name. If anyone runs a background check on you, we'll know about it." He withdrew a sheaf of papers. "The complete dossier on Detective Mike Vargas."

Felicia and Nick scanned the first few pages.

"Not exactly a sterling work record," Felicia observed. "This guy's been written up more times than a juvenile delinquent. Why is he still carryin' a badge?"

"Gotta love police unions," Nick said.

"Got somethin' else for you," McCoy said, then handed Nick a cell phone. "We removed the GPS chip so it's untraceable, but all of your communications will be monitored and recorded. If you talk to Turk on that phone, he might say somethin' incriminating."

"Nice touch," Nick said.

Bones settled into his seat. "I'm kinda hazy on the op you're basin' this on, the one where you went underground before. What was it all about?"

"I was in charge of the London office. We were working with MI6 to stop the flow of illegal weapons. Primarily, we were targeting a guy named O'Halloran. He was the biggest wholesaler in the UK and was doing business with a lot of people on our watchlist. We were going to plant someone inside his organization. Figuring it would take too long to get results, we came up with some competition. We established a rival gunrunner and smuggler named Nick Stavros."

"Deep cover?"

"I was under for more than six months."

McCoy nodded. "You convinced O'Halloran that he should get out while he still could?"

"Something like that. We used our network to undercut his prices and grabbed a lot of his customers. We put him out of business and convinced him to become a snitch."

"Just out of curiosity, what happened to him?"

Nick paused. "I understand he relocated to Venezuela, where his former business contacts wouldn't find him so easily."

"What's the payoff in this caper?"

"Nothing," Nick answered. "It's just what I told you over the phone."

McCoy chuckled. "Sure, that's what you said to get me to help, but you can tell me the whole thing since I'm on board. There's some kind of reward for takin' out Turk Morgan, isn't there?"

"No."

"This Jimmie Rae guy's payin' you somethin' substantial, right?"

Nick shook his head. "Not a dime."

McCoy slowly nodded. "Now I get it. His agent, Brillstein. He put a bounty on Turk to get him off his ass. That's it, right?"

Nick looked at Felicia. "I know I'm talking because I recognize my voice." He addressed McCoy. "There's no payoff, no reward, no hidden treasure, no nothing. We're just doing a favor for a friend. If you want out, I understand."

McCoy was silent for a few moments, then shrugged. "What the hell. Gettin' Turk's people off the streets could be considered a public service. What's the plan?"

"We asked Brillstein to circulate my name among his former clients and to play it up like I'm gunning for Turk. We planted a tracker on his car so we can keep tabs on him. When we get enough info about his organization, we'll start putting the squeeze on him."

"What's my role?"

"Besides recon and tech support, you're the muscle. I haven't paid him a visit yet, but when I do, I expect trouble."

"You should," McCoy said. "I checked out his bodyguard, Antonio Salazar. Real piece of work."

"Police record?" Felicia asked.

He handed them some stapled pages. "Times two. On his last felony arrest, he served two years upstate for assault. He went after a guy with a crowbar and broke both his legs. Shoulda got twelve to twenty. Apparently, he had a good lawyer. Next time he gets busted, he's out of the game. This guy has a black belt, a short fuse, and attitude to spare. A real public menace."

Felicia and Nick looked at Salazar's mug shot. He was deeply tanned, with a bald head, a close-cropped beard, and a barbed wire tattoo around his neck. His rap sheet listed his birthplace as Madrid, Spain, with United States citizenship granted fifteen years earlier.

"It would be beneficial to arrange his arrest," Nick said.

"Won't be easy, since Turk has a cop runnin' interference," McCoy said.

"Yeah," Felicia said. "We should do somethin' about that."

"We will," Nick said. "The rest of the plan depends on our ability to make Turk think he's not the only game in town."

"What's the payoff you're lookin' for?"

"Hopefully to put him out of business," Nick replied. "Jimmie wants Turk off his back, and he wants his girl to come home."

McCoy looked incredulous. "Wait a minute. You're doin'

all this because some guy you know lost his babe to a gang-sta?"

"Partly," Nick said. "Got a problem with that?"

Rolling his eyes, McCoy groaned. "Can't believe I walked into this. Here I thought you were onto somethin' important."

"It is important," Felicia sternly asserted. "You don't think puttin' away a guy who deals drugs and forces young women into prostitution isn't worth your time?" She looked at Nick. "Guess I wasn't wrong about invitin' him to the party, was I?"

"What the hell is that supposed to mean?" McCoy demanded.

"Nick called you because we need your help," Felicia said. "I thought it was a bad idea, but he convinced me you'd do it without expectin' somethin' in return. Was he wrong?"

McCoy's eyes narrowed, and his jaw tensed. "Okay, I'm in. Do you think Turk will buy you as a major player?"

"I think once his rent-a-cop runs the name Nick Stavros, he'll stumble upon the fake cover the CIA put out there twelve years ago," Nick answered. "After we wrapped up that sting in England, Stavros just vanished. He wasn't killed or arrested. According to the official records, he's still out there somewhere."

"You want Turk to think he's here," McCoy said.

"Right. I want him to think I'm Brillstein's silent partner, and I'm highly pissed that he's taking food from my plate."

"Not bad, but there's gotta be somethin' in it for him," McCoy noted. "Somethin' that'll make him want to walk away."

"That's where it gets tricky," Felicia said. "He already has money, a big house in a fancy-ass neighborhood, and a nice public image. What else would a guy like that want?"

"More," Nick said.

Felicia looked at him. "More what?"

"Just more. Have you ever seen a rich, powerful person who didn't want something more? Maybe Turk wants to get a senator elected so he'll have someone influential in his pocket. Maybe Miami isn't a big enough arena for him. Trust me, he wants more." Nick looked into her eyes. "I'm going to offer it to him."

McCoy gave a soft chuckle. "Try this on for size—you're usin' Brillstein's agency as a front for one of your businesses overseas."

"What kind of business?" Felicia asked.

"Recruiting entertainers to work at some clubs you own in Europe, but they're really doubling as couriers. That's why you want Turk to leave Brillstein and his clients alone. If Brillstein gets put out of business, there goes your whole cover operation."

"That's not bad," Felicia concurred. "What will make him take the bait?"

"I could offer him a piece of the operation," Nick said. "Get him to put his own money on the table, and when we have enough proof, we bring in the Feds."

McCoy shook his head. "Needs work. I'm sure the Feds and the cops know all about Turk, but they haven't touched him."

"They probably need a good reason," Nick said. "I'm sure he's paying off the right people to ignore his illegal businesses, but we'll give them something they can't overlook."

"Like ties to a terrorist cell or drug cartel?" Felicia asked.

"Yeah," Nick answered. "The FBI wouldn't look the other way on something like that, especially if it involves national security."

McCoy leaned forward to make some notes on a pad of paper. "Let's work on gettin' your name out there to make Turk think you're the bad-ass you claim to be."

"How?" Nick asked.

"I know some people I can use to spread the word," he replied. "By the time you pay your first visit, he'll know who you are. We'll tweak your phony background, too."

"Like what?" Nick asked.

"If you're usin' Brillstein's clients as mules, you need someplace for them to work. We'll add some clubs in the UK and Japan that are actually fronts for your merchandise."

"Then let's make it really convincing," Nick said. "I'll email you a list of the clients Turk stole from Brillstein. Have someone approach them, claiming to represent me. Offer them overseas jobs that pay more than he's offering."

McCoy stood. "Good idea. Give me a coupla days. In the meantime, look over that stuff I brought you on Vargas. You two can come up with somethin' that'll get internal affairs lookin' up his digestive tract."

Nick showed McCoy out. Felicia drank some coffee and thought. *I still don't like bringin' him in on this. I know he has resources and manpower, but still . . .*

Nick took Felicia's hands, pulled her to her feet, and gave her a firm hug and a kiss.

"What was that for?" she asked.

"For playing him like a Stradivarius. You always know when to say the right things to get someone in line."

Felicia giggled in embarrassment and glanced down. "Stop it."

Nick placed his fingers under her chin and raised her gaze to meet his. "I mean it. You may not realize it, but you've got a real devious streak running through you." He flashed a sly grin. "It's one of the things I've always liked about you."

She ran her fingers through his hair. "I've always thought it was somethin' we had in common. I've seen you play your share of cons, too, but there's somethin' I have to ask."

"Shoot."

"What's up with this whole best bud thing you two have goin'?"

"What do you mean?"

"Whenever you've asked him for help before, he's had some personal angle up his sleeve. One time, he damn near got both of us sent to a federal lock-up. I still don't trust him, and I don't really understand why you do."

Nick ran his fingers along the back of her neck under her long mane of hair. "This might be tough to explain, but I'll try. We both worked in the field, and sometimes you had to rely on people who may or may not have been on the square. You had to trust your gut. Were they telling you the truth or just what they thought you wanted to hear so you would play along? That's kind of how Bones is. Did I trust him when we worked in the field? Not completely but when it came to the showdown with guns drawn, did I think he'd have my back? Definitely. That's how it was." He shrugged. "Sorry if that offends you, but it's how I feel."

She peered into his eyes. "I can live with that, but let's not give him anythin' he can use to his own advantage later."

Nick gave her a quick peck on the lips. "Count on it." He paused before saying, "But, I think we should give him something as a consolation prize."

"Such as?"

"Vargas, the dirty cop."

Felicia laughed in appreciation. "That would keep him busy and away from the real target."

"Great devious minds think alike."

CHAPTER FOUR

Nick and Felicia sat in the back seat of a town car being driven by McCoy. Three days had passed since they'd hatched their scheme to take on Turk Morgan, and the time was right. Felicia had utilized the tracker she planted on Turk's car to learn his schedule and movements. Nick had familiarized himself with everything they could learn about his empire, and McCoy had followed through on making contact with some of his entertainers.

Nick had spent time remembering everything about the deep cover story the CIA had fabricated for the man known to the international criminal community as Nick Stavros, professional mercenary and smuggler. He needed to be prepared in case Turk had done his homework and referenced anything from his so-called past. Nick recalled the checkered pedigree he had lived with for six months undercover. While posing as the weapons trader on the run from the US government, he had lived and worked in Glasgow, Scotland, and established himself as the go-to person for those in need of military-grade artillery. He had also branched into smuggling contraband, from cigarettes without tax stamps to bootleg liquor and uncut gems. When a real gang knocked over a munitions plant in Berlin, the agency had altered the official report to indicate Nick Stavros was responsible. The clerical error further boosted his credibility.

"Did anyone check me out yet?" Nick asked.

"Yeah," Bones answered. "My people said they got a request from Vargas, supposedly on behalf of the Miami Beach

Police."

"That strikes a false note right there," Felicia said. "Cops don't have to use private companies to do background checks."

"Vargas may not be as slick as he thinks," Nick added. "That means we might catch him up in another bungle."

He looked out the window at the throng of people clogging the sidewalks of South Beach. All were dressed in what they thought was the latest party attire, some good, some gauche.

The neon jungle, in all its glory. Party central, Florida's biggest adult playground. If half of the narcotics cops in town weren't on someone's pad, they'd make their quota of arrests in one night.

"What else have you heard?" Nick asked.

"Turk's on the defensive," Bones answered. "He knows who you are but not what you're up to. Accordin' to my sources, he's hit up ev'ryone he knows to find out what he can about you. He's locked and loaded."

Nick stared out the window. "Let's give him his money's worth. You both know what to do?"

"We're ready," Felicia said. "Are you?"

Nick looked at her. "Meaning what?"

"It's been a long time since you went undercover."

Nick gave her a reassuring smile and squeezed her hand. "It's like riding a bicycle."

"You don't have training wheels to break your fall."

"With you along for the ride, I don't need them."

She giggled. "You're sweet, but just be careful in there."

McCoy parked in the lot next to Bahama Joe's. They walked to the entrance. Nick wore a black suit with a pink long-sleeved silk shirt, the top two buttons undone and an inch of cuff extending from his coat sleeves. A Greek Ortho-dox crucifix on a heavy gold chain glistened in the light. He hadn't shaved for the past two days, giving him the gruff look. He donned a pair of rose-hued glasses as they approached the club. He glanced at Felicia.

She had chosen a slinky blue silk cocktail dress with a tropical floral pattern, one that perfectly showed off her natural attributes. The high-heeled leather sandals she wore accented her toned legs, set off by the gold ankle bracelet that spelled out her name. A sterling silver pendant with a diamond angel rested on her bare upper chest.

McCoy was dressed in a black suit over a black long-sleeved shirt that was opened at the neck, showing off a thick gold chain.

Nick laced his arm with Felicia's. He leaned over to speak in a low voice. "Just remember — arm candy, nothing more for the moment."

"I'll behave," she said.

He eyed her again. "By the way, that dress really works for you."

She smiled. "Thank you. The drug dealer wannabe outfit looks good on you, too."

"We should play dress-up more often."

"Your fantasy is mine, tough guy."

They cut to the front of the long line but were stopped by the bouncer. "Got a reservation?"

"Don't need one, *compadre*," Nick said. "I'm on the VIP list."

The bouncer consulted a clipboard. "Name?"

Nick paused for a few seconds. "Stavros. Mr. Morgan is expecting me."

Stepping aside, the man unhooked the barrier rope. "Welcome to Bahama Joe's. Enjoy your evening."

Nick snapped his fingers at McCoy. "Give him a buck for keeping the peasants out."

They entered the crowded club, instantly greeted by deafening music that competed with people laughing. Nick scanned the two-story interior. The wall to his right was a large hand-painted mural depicting a tropical beachfront scene, complete with white sandy beach, blue waves, exotic birds, and partially-nude women. The club's motif was very South Seas, accented by dark wicker furnishings and planters hanging from the ceiling and balcony. An art deco mirrored ball reminiscent of the disco era hung over the dance floor, illuminated by a rotating color wheel mounted somewhere above. The band had just finished their set and were setting their instruments aside. A DJ took over. The tables emptied as customers lay siege to the lighted dance floor, jockeying for space to try their best vertical seduction moves set to music.

The horseshoe-shaped bar, dark teak wood atop glass blocks, took up nearly half of the front club space. He looked up at the wraparound balcony and a smaller bar, surrounded by bistro tables, all occupied by couples taking advantage of the darkened area to focus on each other rather than the music. Nick guided them to the bar.

"Three club sodas with lime," he shouted at the bartender.

When their drinks arrived, Nick scanned the area, spotting Turk Morgan seated at a table in a private alcove toward the back. He was surrounded by four women, two on either side. Three of them were African-American, and the fourth had Hispanic features. They wore fashionable evening attire accented with flashy gold-and-diamond trinkets and well-coiffed hairstyles.

All ready to party the night away, I see. Nick's gaze focused on Jalisa, the one Jimmie had shown him on his cell phone. He also noticed two bodyguards and recognized Salazar from the photo Bones had provided.

He turned and spoke to Felicia. "I see all the players are in attendance. How soon should I make my move?"

She sipped her drink. "Whenever you feel ready."

"I'll give it a few minutes to let the bouncer get word to

Turk that I'm here." Nick peeked over his shoulder. The bouncer was in a huddle with Turk, pointing at Nick. "It's show time."

He stood, picked up his drink, and proceeded to the secluded area where Turk was holding court. He stopped and stared at him through his tinted glasses.

"Is there something I can do for you?" Turk asked.

"Yeah," Nick replied. "You can get your fat ass out of my town."

One of Turk's bodyguards firmly grabbed Nick's arm from behind. Nick whirled around to face the man, dropping his glass. The bodyguard looked down in surprise when it splashed on his feet. Nick took advantage of his distraction to give him a quick uppercut to the chin, knocking him backward. Nick grabbed a fistful of shirt and pulled him forward, delivering a hard right to his jaw, followed by his knee driving into the man's gut. He let out a surprised cry of pain and doubled over, cradling his midsection. A quick chop to the back of his neck sent him crumbling to the floor. He groaned, then lapsed into unconsciousness.

Salazar pulled a Glock nine-millimeter pistol from his waist. Nick quickly withdrew his Walther PPK from his shoulder holster and leveled it at Salazar. He stared at the Spaniard over the barrel. "Nobody calls you a hero until you're dead. Is that how you want this to play out?"

"That will do, Antonio," Turk calmly intoned. "Apparently, Mr. Stavros would like to talk to me."

Nick's gaze scanned the four women. "In private."

Turk addressed the women. "Ladies, would you go amuse yourselves elsewhere for a few minutes?" He looked at Salazar. "You may leave, too, Antonio, and take Spoon with you. When he wakes up, tell him he's fired. Give him two weeks' severance pay." He shifted his gaze to Nick. "My compliments. He came highly recommended."

Nick holstered his gun while the alcove emptied. "It's tough to find good help in a down economy."

Turk gave a gruff chuckle. "Point taken. Please join me."

Nick took a seat and removed his glasses, tucking them into the breast pocket of his jacket. He did a quick but trained scan of the would-be mobster, his tailored gray silk suit, crisp white shirt, and maroon-striped gray tie in a Windsor knot. His gaze picked up the oversized gold nugget diamond rings that adorned a finger on each hand.

Turk indicated a bottle of single-malt Scotch. "Help yourself."

"I never touch the stuff during working hours."

"It's late in the evening. Surely you're off the clock."

"Not in my business."

Turk sipped his drink. "What business would that be?"

Nick leaned forward and rested his left arm on the table. His other hand casually reached into his side coat pocket and withdrew a small listening device with adhesive backing. He affixed it under the table, concealed by a white tablecloth. "I think you know."

"Yes, I know what your business is, Mr. Stavros. What I don't understand is this interest you've taken in my business."

"I wouldn't have taken an interest if you'd stuck to running drugs, women, and buying off politicians. When you infringed on my livelihood, I became interested."

"If you're referring to the musical artists that one of your representatives has approached, I believe they were being mismanaged by a Mr. Brillstein. I merely made them a better offer." He raised his right hand, palm open. "Praise the Lord."

"Actually, they were my clients. I don't appreciate someone grazing on my land without permission."

"I wasn't aware that Mr. Brillstein had a business associate."

"That's why I'm called a silent partner. I'm sure you're familiar with the concept. It's a lot like the arrangement you have with a detective named Vargas."

Turk's eyes narrowed as he stared at Nick. "You seem to have done your research. Are you also aware of the political clout I possess?"

"Of course. I make it a point to know my adversaries."

He chuckled. "Now, now, Mr. Stavros, let's be civil. There's no reason why we can't come to some sort of mutual agreement. Miami is a large enough playground for both of us."

"It's a sandbox compared to where I'm used to playing."

Nick watched him finish his drink and pour another, carefully stopping at the two-finger mark etched inside the cut crystal glass.

"I recall that you're very big in international circles, Mr. Stavros. I seem to remember reading that your specialty was procuring illegal weapons for those in need."

"Only those who could afford my services."

"I stand corrected. What I didn't read in your dossier was why you left that lucrative trade to concentrate on smuggling."

"Less risk, bigger return. Why did you add drug trafficking to your resume?"

He shrugged. "When a good opportunity presents itself, one must be willing to take a chance to achieve success. What sort of arrangement did you have in mind?"

"One that ends with you folding up your tent and setting up shop elsewhere."

Turk shook his head. "I don't like those terms, sir. This is my sandbox, as you put it, and I'm very comfortable here. However, I might be interested in a partnership."

"Such as?"

"I understand that you're interested in my stable of entertainers to work in some of your nightclubs in other countries.

Knowing your reputation, I can also surmise that you wish to use them for some sort of black market activity. Am I on target?"

"Perhaps. Why would you be interested in joining forces?"

"Miami has been good to me, but a smart businessman is always looking for ways to diversify. Perhaps I'd like to play in your sandbox for a while."

Nick gave him a narrowed look for a few moments. "There's an old Greek saying. The man who works best works alone."

Turk gave a gruff chuckle. "We had a similar saying in the neighborhood where I grew up. Don't turn your back on your friends, or you might find a knife in it."

"Say I agreed to a partnership. What would you contribute?"

"You want to use my people as mules, and I'm always interested in making money from my investments. You can figure it out."

Nick stood, reached into his shirt pocket and withdrew a business card with the number of his disposable cell phone on it. He tossed it onto the table.

"Speculation is cheap, but if you want to tender a serious offer, contact me." He looked around the club. "By the way, your establishment is furnished in rather questionable taste." He raised his open palm. "Praise the Lord."

Nick, Felicia, and Bones left the club. Bones drove, merging with the northbound traffic to cut over to Collins Avenue, heading for North Miami Beach. Their drive took them past the iconic Fontainebleau and Eden Roc hotels, once the exclusive domain of sun-worshiping celebrities and wealthy retirees. They were enjoying a resurgence in popularity thanks to the new money crowd that had laid claim to the Treasure

Coast.

"How do you think it went?" Felicia asked.

"I think I've whet his appetite," Nick said. "Did you two pick up on anything while Turk and I were talking?"

"The bodyguard, Salazar," Bones said. "He was talkin' to the other muscle at the bar. I got the feelin' he'd like to go a few rounds with you for pullin' a piece on him and makin' him look like a fool in front of his boss."

"That's just how I wanted him to feel," Nick said.

"Hon, that guy looks like he could give you some serious pain," Felicia said. "Why antagonize him?"

"To get him out of the picture. He's a two-time loser. I want him to go three for three on felony convictions."

They pulled to a stop in the circular drive of a six-story condo complex near Collins Park. A few well-dressed couples exited the building accented by a concrete fountain illuminated by multi-colored lights. The palm trees gently swayed in the evening breeze.

"You're home, sort of," Bones said.

"You're sure this place is secure?"

"We did a sweep this afternoon before you checked in. It's clean. What's next on the agenda?"

"Check with the people you have working the streets. See if Turk bought my charade and call me in the morning."

"Got it. I had someone run a deeper check on Vargas, too. Hopefully, they came up with somethin' we can use. I'll send it to you."

Nick took Felicia's hand to escort her up the steps and into the building, through the white marble lobby to the elevator. They rode to the sixth floor to reach their unit. The living room was fully furnished in coordinated shades of tan and beige, with a couch and two matching chairs adjacent to a kitchenette with an eat-at counter.

Nick crossed to the wet bar and fixed them each a drink

while Felicia made a beeline for the bathroom. He slipped off his jacket and shoulder holster, draping them over a chair. Felicia returned, and Nick held out her glass.

"Shall we have this in the library or on the east terrace?" he asked.

"The terrace, of course. It's much too pretty a night to stay in."

"The terrace it is."

He accompanied her to the balcony overlooking the beach and the ocean. They took seats in the padded chairs, and Nick fired up a cigarette.

Felicia took a sip. "Bringin' back memories?"

"Of what?"

"The times you did this before."

"Yeah, and it's reminding me how much I don't miss it."

They sat in silence for a few minutes, absorbing the night sounds of waves gently lapping on the shore, accompanied by surprised laughter and squeals from people out for a moonlight beach stroll along the water's edge. The half-moon peeked through a few wispy clouds that lazily rolled by, subtly illuminating the stillness.

"Kind of an awesome feelin', lookin' at the big dark beyond out there," Felicia said. "Makes you wonder how far you'd have to go before you found any sign of civilization."

"Uh-huh. Is that the feeling you had on the beaches in Barbados?"

"Sometimes." She tucked a leg under her and settled into the chair. "When I was a teenager, I used to stand out there on nights like this, watchin' ships cruise by or head out of port. I always wondered where they'd been or where they were goin'."

"Is that what prompted you to leave when you turned eighteen?"

"Partly. You know my dad is a retired marine colonel. He

used to tell me stories about all the places he'd been when he was on active duty. It made me want to see some of those places for myself. As soon as I came to the states and got my papers, I joined the corps."

Nick sipped his scotch. "Which part of your life satisfied your wanderlust? The marines or the CIA?"

She looked at him. "Would it surprise you if I said neither?"

"Yeah, it would. There must've been someplace that captured a place in your heart."

Felicia stared into her glass before responding. "I'd have to say England but only for one reason."

"Such as?"

She lifted her gaze to meet his and a smile played across her lips. "That's where I met you."

He leaned over to give her a soft lingering kiss. "It holds special meaning for me, too."

"In spite of how we met?"

Nick hesitated at the memory she dredged up, of his wife being killed in a terrorist bombing meant for him. "Yeah, in spite of what brought us together. You were there for me during my personal darkest hour, and I've never forgotten what you did to bring me back to life." He paused. "I don't know if I ever thanked you for that."

"You did when we got back together a few years later and asked me to stay here with you instead of goin' back home. Best decision I ever made."

"Mine, too."

Felicia took a sip. "Looks like we have the rest of the evenin' to ourselves. What do you want to do?"

Nick looked at her, his playful side coming out of hiding, one reflected in his voice. "What we'd normally do when we're away from home on an overnight."

Felicia gave a seductive chuckle. "You weren't kiddin'

when you said you liked this dress."

"No, I wasn't. Were you kidding when you said you liked what I'm wearing?"

She stood and slinked toward him, giving Nick a smoldering look that was evident in the dim light. She perched on his lap with her legs straddling his and rested her hands on his shoulders. Her gaze bored into his with a look that communicated more than words.

"Mm-hmm," she cooed while undulating against him. "I like it a lot. Wanna know a secret?"

"Sure."

She stood, backed up to the railing a few feet away, and rested her butt against it. She grasped the dress near her waist and slowly gathered up the material, raising it an inch at a time along her toned legs and thighs. Nick's heart beat faster as more of her body was teasingly exposed. His eyes widened a bit when Felicia pulled the fabric over her crotch, revealing that she was *au naturel* under the cocktail dress.

Felicia cocked her right leg to the side. Even in the dimness, Nick could make out her trimmed pubic patch glistening with the dampness of her desire. Felicia moved her hand between her legs and lightly ran her fingers over her sex.

"Like what you see?" she teased while fingering herself.

Nick rose and approached her. Felicia opened her arms, and he stepped into her embrace. She held him firmly, easing her head back. She opened her mouth ever so slightly and ran the tip of her tongue along her lips, giving him a silent invitation. He accepted. The fit of her lips was as perfect as ever, and he could taste the lingering sweetness of strawberry lip gloss. He pressed deeper and lost himself in the kiss until she drew away. She touched a finger to the stubble on his cheek, traced a slow line down his jaw, and gave him a dreamy-eyed gaze with a hint of a smile.

Nick became aware of voices from the beach below. He

took Felicia's hand, led her inside, and closed the balcony drapes. No sooner had he turned around than Felicia was on him like a lynx that had cornered its prey. She pulled him close, forcefully pressing her lips against his. Her tongue invaded his mouth and engaged his in an erotic dance. Nick moved his hands along her back until he reached her firm butt. He pulled her dress up while they kissed until her ass was exposed to fondle and squeezed her cheeks, all while pressing against her, his hard-on straining against his pants.

Felicia pulled back slightly and flashed a teasing look. "Are you carryin' a blackjack in your pocket?"

"No, it's all me."

Taking a step back, she pulled Nick's shirt from the waist of his pants. She unbuttoned it and ran her fingers over his hairy chest, her hands lingering on his firm pecs. Nick reached behind her to unzip her dress to pull it down, exposing her firm, braless breasts. He leaned down to mouth her left breast while his hand tweaked the nipple of her other one into hardness. Felicia gave a soft moan and unfastened Nick's pants, pushing them down over his hips. He stepped back to kick off his shoes and remove his pants and shorts.

Felicia pulled his face to hers and hungrily kissed him while her hand stroked and squeezed him into full hardness. He slipped his hand between her legs and played with her, getting her wet. He slipped two fingers inside her.

Felicia moaned softly through their kiss. She pulled her lips back slightly, panting in lusty anticipation. "Bedroom?"

"Unh-uh," Nick answered, then maneuvered her to one of the padded bar stools at the kitchen counter.

Felicia rested her ass on the edge of the stool and pulled her legs toward her torso, leaving her spread open and her dress hiked up around her waist. Nick stood between her legs and squatted slightly to make up the difference in their height. He guided his stiff prick into her, slowly at first, causing her to gasp.

"Aw, damn, hon. That feels so good."

Hands on her butt, Nick thrust in and out in a steady rhythm. Felicia held onto his shoulders, leaning forward to kiss him while he ravaged her. He squeezed her ass while she ran her hand along his shoulders and the back of his neck, her mouth devouring his in a feeding frenzy. Felicia adjusted her position slightly, leaning back and wrapping her legs around Nick's waist, pulling him closer and deeper.

He continued his back and forth movements. Felicia got wetter the longer he made love to her. Her mouth and tongue worked Nick's mouth while she dug her fingernails into his shoulders. Nick's pulse raced, fueled by Felicia's tightness around him. Her personal scent of arousal wafted to his nose, mixing with her perfume. He felt his imminent climax forming deep within and plunged faster.

He gave a muffled groan through their kiss when his orgasm hit, making him swell deep inside Felicia. He came, his cock spasming a half-dozen times. Felicia let out her own muffled wail when she matched his climax with her own, tightening around him, her vaginal muscles clamping his shaft, making him her prisoner.

After a few moments of slower thrusting and kissing, Nick took his mouth from hers and peered into her eyes, taking deep breaths, getting his pulse back to normal. Felicia's eyes held a dreamy glaze, almost like she was lost in a netherworld. He stayed inside her but eased her back slightly to rest against the counter. He wrapped his arms around her torso and pulled her close. Felicia rested her arms on his shoulders and continued teasing him by contracting and relaxing her pelvic muscles around him.

"Damn, girl," he said. "That was one of the hottest times ever. You were incredible."

Felicia raked her fingertips along his scruffy cheek. "You were pretty turned on yourself, tough guy." She giggled. "Maybe I should wear this dress more often."

CHAPTER FIVE

Nick and Felicia exited the building at 8:00 the next morning. The sky was clear and blue, indicating a nice day for beachcombing and laziness. A slight breeze cooled off the rising temperature. Nick had donned a white linen jacket over khakis and a powder blue shirt, while Felicia had slipped into a sundress with an orange floral print, offset by light leather sandals. They walked toward the street but stopped when Nick heard rapidly approaching footsteps. He turned to face a tall wiry man, wearing a light gray suit with no tie, approaching at a fast pace.

"Hold it right there," the man ordered. He quickly flashed what appeared to be a gold badge. "Face the wall and spread 'em."

Nick eyed him for a moment through his dark glasses before doing as he'd ordered. The man patted him down from shoulder to ankle, not finding a weapon.

"Let's see some ID," the man said.

Nick faced him and took his driver's license from his wallet. The man scrutinized it, then handed it back.

"Is there a problem?" Nick asked.

"We're looking for a man fitting your description who pushed in a liquor store last night."

"In this neighborhood?"

"Go figure. Do you live in this building?"

"Yeah. Unit 612. You can check with the building manager."

"Can you account for your whereabouts last night?"

"What time?"

"Between ten and eleven."

"I was here." Nick jerked his thumb at Felicia. "With her. The security cameras will verify that."

The man stared at Nick for a few moments. "Sorry for the roust. Just doing my job."

"I didn't get a good look at that badge."

The man took his ID from his pocket, holding it open. Nick read the name, Detective Michael Vargas.

"Look, if you want to register a complaint, I'll give you my Captain's name and number," Vargas said.

"That's all right. No one got hurt."

"I appreciate you being so understanding," Vargas said. "You folks have a nice day."

Nick led Felicia across the street to a Cuban bistro. They took seats at one of the sidewalk tables under a bright green-and-white striped umbrella.

"What was that all about?" she asked.

"The welcome wagon. Vargas is letting us know he's around."

"He's still sittin' in his car down the street, watchin' us."

"Maybe I should send him some coffee."

They placed their orders for Huevos Rancheros with coffee and orange juice. Nick scanned the early morning crowd, seeing people emerging from some of the nearby hotels and timeshares, heading for the beach. They were likely tourists, judging from the beach towels, coolers, and inflatable toys they carried. Most of them were wearing wide-brimmed hats and sunglasses.

"Pretty view from our room," Felicia commented. "Ever think of movin' up here?"

"No. It's too busy. Do you want to relocate to Miami Beach?"

She shook her head. "It's pretty, but I can't imagine livin' here. It's too big and too fast. Too many loud, bright things happenin' all at once like it overwhelms you."

"That's why I like the Keys. It's very laid back and casual."

"What else do you like about it?"

"There's a hint of mystery. Everybody's from somewhere else. Do you know there's probably only a few thousand people who were actually born there? The rest got off a plane from Ohio or stepped out of a Winnebago from Jersey. Or made it ashore from Havana in an old Plymouth they converted into a boat."

Felicia giggled. "No wonder you like it."

"What do you mean?"

"You've always been kind of a nomad, driftin' from one place to another, no forwardin' address."

"Is that a bad thing?"

"No, and I know where it came from. When we worked in the field for the CIA, we never knew where we'd be spendin' Christmas one year to the next. It was just somethin' you got used to. Sorta like the marines." She grinned. "Some years, I got deployed to so many different locations, my mail took months to catch up with me. Drove my family crazy, not knowin' where I was or how I was gettin' along."

Their orders arrived, and they began eating.

"What made you decide to settle in Key Largo after you got out of the CIA?" Felicia asked.

"The things you mentioned, plus the anonymity."

"Anonymity?"

"The Keys have more former cops and government agents per capita than anywhere else in the country, but you don't know who they are. The same with the rest of the crowd. Nobody really cares who you are or what you did before you went there."

"Never thought about that, but you're right. I'm amazed at how many regulars we get at the club who know who we are, and we know who they are, but nobody has a last name."

"See what I mean? A hint of mystery."

Nick's cell phone rang. He read the caller ID, then put it on speaker so Felicia could listen in.

"Hey, it's McCoy," Bones said. "You awake?"

"Yeah. Just having breakfast across the street. What's up?"

"After I dropped you two off last night, I doubled back to Turk's club. That bug you planted under his table worked. He's pretty steamed about you makin' a scene on his home turf. He placed a call to his cop buddy, Vargas. Told him to check you out."

"Yeah, he did that as soon as we walked out the front door this morning. He's still watching us. What else did he say?"

"He gave Salazar orders to be on the alert. He must think you're comin' back with reinforcements."

"Did he say anything we can use to get Vargas out of the picture?" Felicia asked.

"Nothin' obvious," McCoy answered. "Turk's been playin' this game for a while, and he knows what not to say. Sounded like he's more interested in what you're up to."

"Then it looks like Vargas is going to be babysitting us today," Felicia said.

"What's the plan?" McCoy asked.

"Keep digging into Turk's operation," Nick said. "There has to be some rock we can look under."

"What're you two gonna do?"

"Felicia was going through that information you sent us on Vargas. We'll keep working on that angle."

"What about Vargas? Turk's gonna expect a report."

"He'll get one. We'll hang around here today, maybe hit the beach like the other tourists."

McCoy laughed. "Sure, live it up on my dime."

"We need to blend in. Swing by here tonight around seven. We'll visit one of Turk's other clubs. Call me if anything else happens."

He disconnected, and they finished eating.

"Why the low-key approach?" Felicia asked.

"To give Turk a reason to stay up nights. He must think I'm someone to be taken seriously or he wouldn't have reached out to Vargas. In a situation like this, it wouldn't make sense for me to go around busting heads as soon as I hit town. A first-class operator like Nick Stavros would take his time to get the lay of the land and plan a counter-strike."

"That's what's gonna keep Turk awake and restless?"

"That's right."

Felicia sipped her coffee. "It could work, I guess."

Nick eyed her for a moment. "I'm sensing a bit of reluctance in your tone this morning. Something you want to talk about?"

Felicia glanced down. "I just don't want this to become a regular thing, for either of us."

Nick took her hand. "Do you really think I want to get back into the spy game?"

"No, but I don't want anything to upset what we have goin'."

Nick chuckled. "I never thought it was possible."

"What?"

"You're selfish."

Felicia's gaze locked onto his. "Damn right, I'm selfish. I waited a long time for this. We worked together in England when you were married, I was there for you after your wife got killed, I missed you when you quit the agency, and when we finally reconnected a few years ago, I couldn't believe my sudden good fortune. When you asked me to stay here with you, I thought I'd hit the jackpot. You think I'm givin' all that up?"

Nick laughed and squeezed her hand. "What do you know? Miss Kill-or-be-killed has a heart and soul."

Felicia gave an embarrassed grin. "That runs both ways, tough guy. You've made a career out of keepin' your feelings in cold storage."

"And it took you to thaw them out." He paused. "Thank you."

She brought his hand to her lips and kissed it. "My pleasure. What do we do now?"

Nick took out his wallet to pay the bill. "Let's act like a couple of tourists."

They strolled along Collins Avenue, visiting a few high-end boutiques and shops. An hour later they were back in their condo. Nick noticed that Vargas had maintained his post.

"I wonder what excuse he gave his Captain for pulling stakeout duty on someone who isn't wanted for anything," Nick said.

"He probably pulled your old sheet and claimed that you're a person of interest," Felicia said.

"If he thought that, he would've called in the FBI. What did you dig out of his file?"

Felicia opened a notebook. "I found a half-dozen complaints to the Citizen's Review Board. They're a watchdog group the cops formed to make it look like they care about their public image."

"Man, you're cynical."

"I got it from you. The complaints alleged that Vargas used unnecessary force and harassed innocent people to make his cases. One of the complainants claimed that Vargas extorted money so he wouldn't be arrested for dealin' drugs."

Nick sat in one of the chairs. "Sounds promising. What was the outcome?"

"Charge dismissed because the guy had a record."

"That's an old, dirty cop trick. Shakedown the criminals

because they're not likely to bitch. Does it say who the target was?"

Felicia consulted the page. "Joseph Montero. Filed the complaint a year ago."

"Which means he's probably still around. We'll get McCoy to run it down."

"You think this guy will play along?"

"He tried to get Vargas off his back through legitimate channels, and it didn't work. Anything else noteworthy?"

"Accordin' to this, Vargas lives in Coral Gables and has a boat moored at a marina near Matheson Hammock."

"Coral Gables. Not exactly the poor side of town. What kind of boat?"

Felicia looked at the page. "A Bayliner cabin cruiser."

"The man has good taste."

Felicia shook her head. "You guys and your boats. He also has a timeshare in Key West and an ex-wife collectin' a lot of alimony."

"That makes Vargas the perfect cop on the take."

"How do you figure that?"

"A civil servant with expensive tastes and an ex who raked him over the coals in the divorce. Guys like Turk look for someone who has a lot of overhead, like alimony, a kid's college tuition, or a house they can't afford."

She set the notebook on the table. "That's all the juicy stuff. What do you think is the best way to get this cop out of the way?"

Nick thought for a few moments. "What if we got him on video accepting a bribe?"

"From who?"

"That Montero guy. We could set up a sting."

"Might work, but that's only one problem."

"What's the other one?"

"Salazar. I don't like the idea of you goin' one-on-one with him. He looks mean."

"He probably is. Got an idea?"

She shook her head. "Not yet. I want to study him more first."

Nick stood. "While you're thinking about it, want to hit the beach?"

Nick swam through the incoming current to catch up with Felicia, who had bested him after they dived into the ocean. When he reached her, he treaded water, shook his head, and spat out the mouthful of the Atlantic he had sucked in. Felicia bobbed neck high, treading water while giving him a teasing smile. Nick sidled up next to her and brushed his wet hair back from his face.

"Looks like I win, tough guy," she proclaimed. "Five bucks. Pay up."

"I left my wallet in my other pants."

They floated with the gentle tides and looked around. Several sailboats coasted in the distance, along with some jet skis out for a day of exploring. The white sandy beach was dotted with bikinied sun worshipers and a group playing volleyball. The smell of saltwater and sunscreen permeated the air, punctuated by excited cheers and chatter from the volleyball crowd.

"Sure is pretty out here," she said.

"That's the second time you've said that. Are you sure you're not trying to tell me something?"

She splashed water in his face. "No, I'm not tryin' to tell you anythin'. Can't a person make an observation without you readin' somethin' into it?"

"Old habit."

She pulled him in for a kiss. "Get over it."

Her long wet hair dangled carelessly around her face. He

peered into her eyes while caressing her cheek. "Felicia, I'd be happy anywhere we lived as long as you were there. I just can't envision life without you being a part of it."

She gave him a dreamy smile. "Now who's bein' selfish?"

"Come on. I'll race you back to shore."

"Double or nothin'?"

"You're on."

They swam toward the beach, coasting part way on the waves and reached the sandbar at the same time. They walked onto the beach and caught their breath.

"Tie," Nick declared.

"You still owe me five bucks."

They walked to where they had laid out their towels, and Nick took two bottles of water from the beach bag. He handed one to Felicia, then took a long drink.

"I see our watchdog is still on the job," he said.

"Where is he?"

"At the concession stand behind us. I hope he isn't collecting overtime for this."

Nick let his gaze wander over Felicia's toned body, her bronze skin offset by a white mesh bikini that clung to her body. Rivulets of water dripped from her hair when she fluffed it with her fingers. In spite of the heat, her nipples pressed against her bikini top.

"I guess that water was cooler than it looks," he said.

"What do you mean?"

He indicated her breasts. "You're standing at attention."

She moved a step closer to run her fingers along his arm. "If we were back home on Barbados, I wouldn't be wearin' this."

"We should plan a trip there."

They stretched out on a couple of lounges to let the sun dry them off. The breeze gently wafted in, making the palms sway. The quiet was punctuated by a family nearby with the sounds of giggling children building sandcastles adding a touristy counterpart. Nick closed his eyes and began to relax but was soon interrupted by a volleyball landing on his gut. His eyes snapped open and he spied a teenaged girl in cutoff jean shorts and a bikini top, standing nearby with her hand on one hip, giving him a challenging look.

"Hey, mister," she said. "You gonna throw my ball back or what?"

Nick stood and palmed the volleyball. He drove his fist into it, sending it sailing over the net. The other team scrambled to retrieve it.

The girl looked at him with wide eyes and a big smile. "Wow! Wanna come play for our team?"

Nick waved her off. "Some other time."

He reclined on the chaise.

Felicia chuckled. "Looks like you could have a second career as a volleyball beach bum."

"Nice to know I have something to fall back on."

Felicia took a drink of water. "You said somethin' when we were in Brillstein's office the other day, about doin' this because you don't like bullies."

"What about it?"

"I think that explains a lot about you. Have you always been that way?"

"I've encountered my share of them, but who hasn't? There probably isn't anyone who didn't get pushed around on the playground when they were a kid. I just learned how to stand up to them."

"Did you ever do that for someone else?"

Nick gazed absently at the ocean, listening to the zoom of jet skis passing too close to shore. He heard a high-pitched scream, followed by the hearty laughter of someone who had thrown someone else into the water unexpectedly. From further down the beach, the sounds of an old Rolling Stones song drifted in.

"Yeah. You know I had a younger sister."

"She got killed with your parents in a car accident when you were a senior in high school, right?"

Nick nodded. "She was two years younger than me. There was this guy in her class who picked on her. You know how cruel kids can be at that age, and he did some pretty mean stuff, like calling her unflattering nicknames and messing with her art projects. I thought she was really upset so I told him to lay off. We got into it, and I popped him in the face."

"You were bein' a protective big brother."

"She didn't see it that way. Turns out she had a crush on the guy and got mad as hell because I broke up her big romance." He hesitated. "Shortly after that, she and my parents were killed by a drunk driver. For the longest time, all I could think about was that she was still pissed at me, and I never had the guts to say I'm sorry, Cindy."

"You got over it?"

He looked at her. "Not completely, but it taught me an important lesson about life. Be careful what you say to someone you care about because it may be the last thing you ever say to them."

"Sounds like you grew up fast."

"I didn't have much choice." He stood. "Let's go upstairs. It's getting too hot out here."

When they were in their unit Nick checked his phone for messages and found one from McCoy. He called him back.

"Hey, it's me. You called?"

"Yeah. I found that Montero guy you texted me about. He hangs out on the strip in South Beach, around the Victor Hotel."

"Dealer?"

"Yeah, and accordin' to my sources, he ain't the only one

Vargas is puttin' the bite on."

"How much is he shaking people down for?"

"Coupla hundred a week for protection."

"We need to get him on tape. Do you think we can arrange it with Montero?"

"It's possible. What's on for tonight?"

"I want to check out Turk's other clubs and see if any of Brillstein's former clients are working tonight. We'll pay a visit so I can make my sales pitch in person."

CHAPTER SIX

Nick and Felicia settled into the back seat of the town car. Dusk had fallen over Miami Beach, and the setting sun against the buildings cast long shadows on the sidewalks. The street was a steady flow of traffic heading south, filled with people itching to satisfy their party fix on the beach.

"Where to?" McCoy asked.

Nick handed him a piece of paper. "Club Masquerade in Coconut Grove. That's the address. I checked their website and one of Brillstein's former clients is headlining there tonight."

"Which one?"

"China Peters. He's a drag queen that Turk stole."

McCoy glanced over his shoulder with arched eyebrows. "You want us to go to a gay bar?"

"Their website said everyone is welcome. If you feel uncomfortable, just tell any interested parties that you're with me."

"What about me?" Felicia asked.

Nick looked at her with a grin. "I'll say you're my wing woman."

She scoffed. "Small comfort. What if someone hits on me?"

"Are you really that self-centered?"

"What do you mean?"

"You're assuming someone would hit on you. Maybe they won't."

Felicia gave him a defiant look. "You don't think anyone would find me attractive enough to hit on? I've had plenty of same-sex offers. I just never accepted them."

Nick shook his head. "The longer we're together, the more I learn about you."

She rested her hand on his knee. "Plenty more secrets for you to uncover, tough guy."

"I love a challenge."

"Not to break up this lovefest, but what are you gonna say to this drag queen?" McCoy asked.

"I'll make him an incredible offer, he'll tell Turk about it, and with any luck, Turk will send Salazar after me."

"Pretty high risk," McCoy said. "Salazar plays rough."

"That's what I'm counting on."

McCoy put the car in gear and merged with the southbound traffic. They rode in silence for a few minutes.

"I hate to tell you this, but we picked up a tail," McCoy said.

"Dark blue Ford sedan?" Nick asked.

"Uh-huh. Vargas?"

"That's the car he was using earlier."

"He's been on your ass all day?"

"Since early this morning," Nick confirmed. "We didn't give him much to report. Maybe he thinks he'll strike gold tonight."

"He works for the Miami Beach PD," Felicia said. "What does he hope to accomplish in Coconut Grove since that's out of his jurisdiction?"

"Observe and report," Nick said.

An hour later, they arrived at Club Masquerade, where the flashing pink and yellow neon sign illuminated the people lingering on the sidewalk. They went inside, then found a table. Nick looked around the partially filled, dimly lit club, observing the mix of men and women coupled up. Several loveseats were positioned in the darkened corners of the room, and Nick could make out the couples seated there, some embracing while enjoying the floor show, others engaging in public displays of affection. The overall décor was a palette of muted pastels and low-level perimeter lighting, all done up in a tropical motif, a stark contrast from the blatant sexual overtones of Bahama Joe's.

His attention went to the stage where China Peters was performing, belting out a medley of Barbra Streisand standards. A skinny blonde waitress came by to take their orders. Nick caught the gleam in her eye and trace of a smile when she looked at Felicia.

"Tell the singer I'd like to talk to her when she finishes her set," Nick said.

"Who wants to see her?" she asked.

Nick took some folded money from his pocket, peeled off a twenty, and handed it to her. "Mr. Jackson would like a word with her."

She tucked the twenty into her halter top. "I'll deliver the message personally."

She returned with their drinks. Nick sipped his club soda and listened to China finish her set to loud applause. She went backstage for a few minutes, then made her way to their table. Nick stood as she approached.

"You wanted to see me?" she asked.

"Please have a seat."

Nick sat while he did a scan of her elaborate make-up and shiny light blue sequined cocktail dress. *Even up close, I can't really tell.* "You have a nice act and a lovely voice. Very well-suited for your material."

China flashed a bright smile. "Thank you. Are you a fan?"

"I've never seen you perform before tonight, but I've heard of you. I understand you have quite a following."

"I do all right, I suppose."

Nick took a drink. "How would you like to do better?"

China eyed him with curiosity. "What did you have in

mind?"

"I own a number of nightclubs overseas. A talent like yours would go over very well in, say, Tokyo or London."

Her eyes widened. "Are you serious?"

"Very."

"I'm flattered, but I couldn't possibly leave Miami."

Nick hesitated a beat. "You mean you couldn't possibly leave Turk Morgan?"

Her painted eyelids narrowed. "Your name wouldn't be Stavros, would it?"

"It would."

She stood. "I can't be seen talking with you."

"Has Turk put the fear into you?" Felicia asked.

China looked at her. "Let's just say I don't want to end up with a face full of acid. That seems to be how he handles employee disputes."

"I can provide protection," Nick said. "And I'll double what he's paying you to work here." He handed her a business card. "Think it over."

China quickly disappeared backstage. A DJ took over the stage and people converged on the dance floor.

"Think that did any good?" Felicia asked.

"I think she's probably on the phone to Turk as we speak," Nick answered, glancing at the bar. "Vargas is still with us."

"Man, he sure is sloppy when it comes to surveillance," Bones commented. "No way we should've spotted him. What that singer just said. Guess Turk's a bigger badass than I thought."

"He plays for keeps," Felicia said.

"Then we need to do somethin' about him," McCoy said.

Nick looked curiously at him. "Sounds like you're buying into the program."

"I don't like what he's doin', and he needs to get knocked down a few pegs. What's next on the agenda?"

"Let's go to South Beach and find that drug dealer, Montero," Nick said. "First, we're going to leave Vargas in the dust."

They made their way toward the exit. Nick took a detour to the bar, stood near Vargas and leaned in close.

"You're a little out of your jurisdiction, aren't you?" he asked. "Miami Beach is your beat."

Vargas gave him a narrowed sideways look. "You talkin' to me?"

Nick chuckled. "That's very Robert De Niro, but he had a little more swagger in his delivery. Work on that."

Vargas sipped his beer. "I'm just enjoying a quiet drink. What's it to you?"

"You don't seem like the type to hang out in a joint like this. I guess if your buddies saw you in one of these clubs on South Beach, it'd be difficult to explain in the locker room, huh?"

Vargas's narrowed squint locked onto Nick's eyes. "You have something you want to say, Stavros?"

"Yeah. If I didn't know better, I'd think you were following me."

Vargas smirked. "Don't flatter yourself."

"Right. That's why you were pulling ass duty all day, sitting outside my building, then following me down here."

Vargas turned to face him. "I should run you in."

"For what? I haven't done anything illegal, and you have no standing here." He stood upright. "Tell Turk I said hi."

Nick rejoined Felicia and McCoy at the door. When they reached the parking lot, Nick found Vargas's car. He looked around the immediate area before he took a knife from his pocket. He opened it, punctured the right front tire, then joined Bones and Felicia in the car.

"What was all that at the bar?" Felicia asked.

"Just letting Vargas know that I'm on to him."

"I'll bet when you were a kid, you liked to poke beehives with a stick."

"Part of my misspent youth."

An hour later, they were parked in a public lot on Ocean Drive. They walked along the sidewalk on the waterfront side, dodging people going to the beach, visiting the open-air art gallery or stopping at some of the pop-up stands selling cheap souvenirs and snow cones. Nick stopped when he spied a familiar figure across the street rapidly walking in the direction of Bahama Joe's.

"Isn't that Jimmie?" Felicia asked.

"Yeah," Nick replied. "What the hell is he doing here?"

"The way he's walkin', he looks like he's on a mission."

Nick dodged the traffic as he ran across the street, pushing his way through the crowd like a fish swimming upstream. He caught up with Jimmie Rae and grabbed his arm, pulling him into an alley. He shoved his back against a building and bored into his eyes.

"What the hell are you up to?" he demanded.

"I'm goin' to see Turk and have it out with him."

"Why now?"

"He called me. Asked if I was ready to come work for him, and when I told him no, he threatened Jalisa."

Nick took a step back. "Threatened her how?"

"He said a fine lady like her would be a big hit with his hip-hop and gangsta rapper buddies. Said they'd pass her around like a party favor. He said if that didn't make me come around to his way of thinkin', I should remember the name Jasmine Blake."

"You know what happened to her?"

"Damn straight. Brillstein told me."

Nick looked him up and down, then held out his hand. "Let's have the piece."

"What piece?"

"The one tucked into your waistband. Hand it over."

Jimmie paused for a few moments, then withdrew a .38 revolver.

Nick slipped it into his jacket pocket. "Confronting Turk on his home turf isn't the way to go. Salazar would nail your ass as soon as you walked through the door."

"You got somethin' better?"

"Yeah, and I'm working on it. I just need you to stay out of the way."

"What do I do about Jalisa?"

Nick thought for a moment. "Call Turk and tell him you'll work for him."

Jimmie defiantly shook his head. "No way, Nick. That crook ain't gettin' his claws into me again."

"Would you rather he carried out his threat against your girl? If Turk thinks you're playing along, he'll leave you and Jalisa alone. That should take some of the pressure off of you."

"Will this plan you're workin' on get Turk off my back?"

"I'm gonna do my best. Be sure you don't tell anyone about what I'm doing, and that includes Jalisa."

"I hear ya."

Nick placed his hand on Jimmie's shoulder. "Good. Now get out of here before someone recognizes you."

Nick watched Jimmie walk back the way he had come, keeping him within sight until he disappeared in the crowd. *Crazy fool. What was he thinking?*

He waited for a break in the traffic, then sprinted across the street.

"What was that all about?" Felicia asked.

"He came gunning for Turk."

"By himself?" Bones incredulously asked. "Even I'm not that careless."

"Love makes you do crazy things," Nick said. "We need to change our game plan. Let's go back to the condo."

CHAPTER SEVEN

Nick stared into the clear night sky through the partially-opened balcony curtain. He took a sip of scotch, closed the curtain, then paced the length of the living room, back and forth. Felicia sat in one of the chairs while Bones slumped on the couch, his long legs stretched out in front of him with his feet resting on the coffee table.

"Hon, will you stop with the pacing?" Felicia said. "You're makin' me dizzy."

"It helps me think," Nick said while continuing to walk. "This subtle approach isn't working. Turk has everyone too scared to jump ship, and he knows it. There has to be some way we can smack him upside the head and get his attention."

"Look, man," Bones said, "you already told your friend Jimmie to give it up and work for him. That's what Turk wants."

Nick stopped pacing and looked at both of them. "That's what he wants for now, but what did I say about him wanting more? What else do we know about his organization?"

"Just what I told you before," Felicia said. "It doesn't look like there's any way to connect him to the money he makes through his illegal businesses."

"That's the key piece. In our collective experience dealing with smugglers and other assorted thieves, what's the one common thread?"

"They never touch the money," Felicia answered.

"Right. They never touch the money. Bones, what else did you find out about Salazar?"

"He's the muscle," Bones replied. "What else is there?"

"What do you want to bet that he's the bag man, the collector?"

"That would make sense," Bones concurred. "If he is, how do we use it to our advantage?"

"Let's think it through," Nick said. "This is no different than any other syndicate or cartel we investigated. They were all in it to make money, but what's the one thing they all counted on?"

"Loyalty," Felicia answered. "It was bought and paid for, but they expected their crew to be somewhat trustworthy."

"That's right," Nick said. "Morals are morals, but money is money. Show me one kingpin who wouldn't get mad if someone he trusted was helping himself to the stash."

Bones pointed his finger at him. "I think I see where you're goin' with this. We make him think someone on the inside is rippin' him off."

"Not just someone," Nick countered. "Salazar."

Felicia laughed. "Seriously? How're we gonna do that?"

"Bear with me. Bones, in that shiny building where your high-tech security firm is located, do you have a computer tech who's smart enough to move money without getting caught?"

Bones gave him a wary gaze. "Possibly, but I run a legit business, and I have several government defense contractors as clients. If they found out, they'd bail and probably turn me in."

"I won't say anything if you don't."

Bones looked down for a few moments. "I've got a guy."

"How long would it take to set up a bank account in Salazar's name and move some of Turk's cash into it?"

Bones shrugged. "Maybe a day, maybe less."

"You set up Salazar as the fall guy," Felicia said. "Then what?"

"We convince Turk that his number one boy has gone independent." He addressed Bones. "Make it look like Salazar's been helping himself to small amounts over a long period of time, not enough to alert the accountants but enough to make a nice nest egg."

"This might work," Bones said. "Say we do set it up. How do we convince Turk that Salazar's been plannin' an early retirement?"

Nick sat in a chair across from him. "I'll let him think I'm interested in taking him on as a partner, provided he can convince me of his net worth, to show he's a good risk. He'll take a look at the books, find the shortage, and follow the money trail."

"That might get Salazar out of the way," Felicia asked, "but how does it put Turk out of business?"

"While Bones is messing with his bank accounts, we'll start some online chatter. You know the Feds are always monitoring internet communications for certain buzzwords."

"To do that, you'd need to hack Turk's e-mail," Bones said. "That's tougher than gettin' into his bank account."

Nick took a drink. "There must be some way we can get something to use against him."

McCoy dropped his feet on the floor, sitting up straight. "What about his credit card statements? A guy like Turk probably puts his life on the company plastic."

"It's worth a look," Nick said.

"Hold it," Felicia said. "I think I have a better idea, one that'll take out two of our biggest problems. Why not set up Vargas as the embezzler? When Turk finds out, he'll send Salazar to break Vargas's legs or worse. We tip off the cops when it's goin' down, they arrest Salazar as a three-time loser, and take a close look at Vargas."

"I like it, but there's one little problem," Nick said. "Vargas is the outside man, and he wouldn't have access to Turk's accounts. Salazar is his right hand."

"I guess you're right," Felicia concurred.

Nick addressed Bones. "While your guy is funneling money into an offshore account, have him give us some for operating capital."

"What kind of capital do we need?" Bones asked.

"We're going to make Vargas look dirtier than he already is, and for that, we need cash."

CHAPTER EIGHT

Felicia sat on the couch the next morning, working on the laptop between sips of coffee. McCoy had come through with Turk Morgan's credit card statements for the past six months, and she reviewed every transaction.

Coulda sworn the Feds went after some Swedish guy for doin' this a few years ago, but now we're doin' it on the sly. Not even for God and country, just to get some hood off the streets. I don't mind the outcome, but the method bothers me. I sure would hate it if I found out someone was trackin' my spending habits and online activity.

Nick joined her from the balcony, carrying a cup of coffee.

"Anything good?" he asked.

"Turk has expensive tastes. Once a week he places an order with a florist in Kendall. A dozen red roses every time."

"What else?"

"Accounts at a high-end jewelry store and some boutiques in Miami Beach."

Nick sat in one of the chairs. "Bling and fancy dresses for his stable of hookers?"

"Maybe the ones who work in his clubs, but I never saw a streetwalker showin' off a Cartier bracelet and Dior evening clothes. Didn't Brillstein say somethin' about Turk droppin' expensive gifts on the women he recruited?"

Nick thought for a moment. "Yeah, and didn't I read that he and his wife are separated?"

"Maybe this stuff is for his girlfriend."

"Or girlfriends. A guy like him probably has more than one

filly on the side."

Felicia looked at him. "You do know what we're doin' is technically against the law, don't you?"

"I'm aware of that."

"It doesn't bother you?"

"Slightly. Does it bother you?"

She went back to her work. "More than slightly."

"Is it because we're peeking in on someone's private life or because you don't like what we're trying to do?"

"I just think people should be allowed to keep their private lives private, no matter who they are."

"I agree but let me hit you with one. Over the past twenty years, everyone has had to sacrifice a part of their privacy. You can't go anywhere without being captured on a security camera, traffic cam, or someone's cell phone. Would you agree?"

"Agreed, but what's your point?"

"The police have used those moments captured in time to solve or prevent a lot of crimes. Sometimes people didn't even know they were doing it. They just took a picture or a video and didn't realize what they had until someone asked them for it."

"Okay, I know we do the same thing at our club with the security cameras, but we never use it to shake someone down, even though we could. We both know that a lot of those couples who come in are married to someone else."

"We don't do anything with it because it wouldn't be right. I'm not advocating for Big Brother, but if they use a red-light video to nail a drunk driver or apprehend someone fleeing the scene after they rob a store, I'm all for it. What's wrong with gathering evidence on someone who's involved in criminal activity?"

Felicia sipped her coffee. "I just feel like a cyber-stalker."

"Private security companies like McCoy's do it all the time

for money."

"One more reason for me not to trust him. Haven't you ever sent an e-mail or text to someone and hoped that no one else would read it?"

Nick paused. "Yeah. Haven't you?"

"Of course. Never anything bad but there have been things I've said digitally that could've been taken out of context. What if all this stuff we're diggin' up on Turk is harmless? We have no way of knowin' that he's supportin' a coupla girlfriends. It's all circumstantial."

Nick drank some coffee. "Would you feel better if we dropped this whole thing and went home?"

She thought for a moment. "No, I want to see it through."

"Okay, but only if you're sure. I don't want you doing something you don't feel comfortable with. Anything else happening?"

"McCoy sent a message that his guy tapped Turk's reserves and set up an account in the Cayman's in Salazar's name. He also moved twenty grand onto that credit card he gave you to use."

"That should be enough for what I have in mind."

"Feel like sharin'?"

"We're going to upgrade Vargas's set of wheels."

Nick and Felicia took a cab to Elite Motorworks in Coral Gables. They had shaken Vargas earlier by having McCoy pick them up, taking them to a restaurant off the strip. Nick and Felicia had slipped out through the service entrance and caught a cab. They got out when they arrived at their destination and strolled through the lot, filled with shiny sports cars and luxury imports.

"Are you sure this guy is trustworthy?" Felicia asked.

"He's a former Key West cop who was moonlighting as a

repo man before he opened this place."

"How does that make him reliable?"

"I did him a favor once upon a time. He got jammed up with a repo client who wouldn't pay up, and I made sure he got his cut."

"I'm not gonna ask how."

"Smart girl."

They entered the showroom, and Nick requested to speak with the owner. Felicia looked out the showroom window at the high-end autos on display.

"Where does he get all these?" she asked.

"Mostly at auctions from car rental companies, but some were repossessed. You'll recognize him when you see him. He's a regular at Cricket's."

Several minutes later, Al Sterling, tall and tanned in casual clothing, approached with a smile and an outstretched hand. "To what do I owe the pleasure, Nick?" he began.

"I need a favor," Nick replied. "I want to rent a car but not in my name. Can you handle that?"

Sterling gave him a wary gaze. "This sounds like the kind of favor the cops wouldn't look too kindly on. What gives?"

"Is there somewhere private we can talk?"

Sterling indicated his office. "In there."

They entered the office, and Sterling closed the door before sitting behind his desk. "What's this all about?"

"We're helping a friend out of a jam, and to do that, we need to get someone out of the way. The guy in question is a crooked cop, and I need it to be obvious that he's living well above his means."

Sterling nodded. "You want to outfit him with a fancy ride, one that his superiors might question."

"You got it. Can it be done?"

"Anything's possible. Who's the actual lessee?"

"Millennium Security. I want to put the car on their corporate account but with a different name on the paperwork."

"I think we can handle that. Which car did you have in mind?"

"On the way in here, I noticed a blue BMW Z4 roadster, a convertible."

"You've got good taste. Got a name and address on the pigeon you're setting up?"

Nick handed him a greeting card in an envelope. "You'll find everything in there. I want the car delivered to his home address with the paperwork in this card, and make sure they hand it over personally. Can that be done?"

"Shouldn't be a problem. How long do you need the car?"

"I think two weeks will be long enough."

They waited while Sterling began the paperwork and charged the car to Nick's credit card. When they were finished, Nick and Felicia got into the waiting cab to go back to South Beach.

"What did you put on the card to make Vargas think Turk treated him to a sports car?"

"I wrote in appreciation of your hard work and dedication. I doubt Vargas will think it came from his boss at the precinct."

Felicia chuckled. "Then what?"

"I visit Turk and raise some questions about the new car Vargas is tooling around in. That'll plant the seeds of doubt." He took out his phone and punched in McCoy's number. "We're on our way back. Any action on your end?"

"Nah, Vargas is sittin' across the street, lookin' bored. Surprised someone doesn't question why he isn't makin' arrests instead of followin' you around."

"Makes you wonder. See you in a few." He disconnected. "Vargas is still pulling stakeout duty."

The cab dropped them off at the alley behind the restaurant. They went in through the kitchen where Nick slipped the chef a twenty. Exiting through the front door, they joined McCoy at the car. They got into the back seat.

"Did you get everything taken care of?" Bones asked.

"We're off to the races," Nick replied.

"Would you mind stoppin' at McDonald's on the way back?" Felicia asked.

"What for?" Nick said.

"You took me to lunch, but we didn't eat. I'm hungry."

CHAPTER NINE

Nick, Felicia, and Bones approached Bahama Joe's just after sunset. All of the clubs and restaurants on the beach were filled to capacity, some with lines of people waiting their turn. Nick guided them to the head of the line. He looked at the bouncer, the same one they had encountered a few nights earlier.

"Do we have to go through formalities again, or are you going to let us in?" Nick asked.

He unhooked the barrier rope, stepping aside. They entered the crowded club, eyeing the well-dressed partiers. Nick scanned the bar and surrounding area. He didn't see Jalisa.

Felicia and Bones went to the bar while Nick proceeded to Turk's private table. He was seated alone and talking on his cell phone but cut his conversation short when he saw Nick standing in front of him. Nick eyed a tall well-muscled black man in dark clothing standing nearby. The man made a move in his direction, but Turk held up his hand.

"Not now, Rico. Mr. Stavros and I have some business to discuss. Leave us."

Nick sat, then looked around. "Where's your boy, Salazar?"

"Running an errand. I understand you've been busy, talking to my employees."

"Good news travels fast."

Turk sipped his drink. "What is it this time, Mr. Stavros?

More posturing about your position in the international market?" He grinned. "Perhaps you've dropped in to tell me you've decided to go back to your base of operations in Glasgow."

"My compliments on your research. Scotland's a great country, but this time of year, the nights are too cold. I like it here."

"You were correct about my research. I've discovered a great deal about you. For example, I learned that not only are you a person of interest to Interpol, but you had to keep your base of operations in the United Kingdom because your own native Greece declined you a visa to enter their country."

Nick chuckled. "Despite common myth, some government officials can't be bought. Actually, I came here to discuss a business proposition."

"Turk is listening."

"I thought about what you said the other night, about Miami being a big enough playground for two bullies. I might be interested."

"Might be?"

"I've checked you out, too, and I have some concerns about your financial well-being."

Turk's gaze narrowed, and his jaw tensed up. "Why should that be any of your business?"

"Whenever I consider taking on a new partner, I check them out. I'm sure you do the same thing."

Turk sat back in his seat and clasped his hands on the table, giving Nick a penetrating stare. "What did you discover that raised a red flag?"

"Several things. The most pressing question is why you're paying that cop of yours so much money to be your gopher."

"Assuming I know what you're referring to, why would you wonder such a thing?"

Nick shrugged. "Because anyone on my payroll only gets

enough to wet their beaks, not take a bath." He paused. "Have you noticed what your pay-for-play detective is driving these days? None of my people could afford a shiny new sports car."

Turk quickly downed his drink, then poured a refill. "I have no idea what you're talking about. Next item on the agenda."

"I checked out this money-laundering operation of yours, and I have one word—sloppy. Running your take through a charity is a nice cover, but you need a couple of buffers in place. The way you're set up, the IRS wouldn't have much trouble making a case for tax evasion. I'd suggest a couple of shell corporations with foreign assets. It's easier to hide the cash that way."

Turk gave a gruff chuckle. "It appears that I'm in the presence of a financial wizard."

"Only one who hasn't been caught yet and doesn't plan to be."

"I assume you have the international connections to make such transactions possible?"

"Could be." Nick hesitated a few seconds. "Not to sound impertinent, but how trustworthy is Salazar?"

"Why do you ask?"

"I checked his police record. A guy like that might be more of a hindrance than an asset. I wouldn't want my share of the profits endangered by a hot-head who can't keep his emotions in check."

"Antonio has been with me for many years, and I trust him with my life." He raised his palm. "Praise the Lord. Next question."

"Whenever I set up a new network, I always bullet-proof my ass ahead of time. What kind of political protection would you be able to offer?"

Turk's gaze narrowed again. "Are you implying that I'm

careless with the precautions I take?"

Nick shook his head. "I'm just pointing out that your operation is local. You want to get into the international market. Once you do that, you're inviting scrutiny from customs, the DEA, and the FBI, among others. Some local hack wouldn't have the juice to run interference with the Feds."

Turk exhaled a slow deep breath. "I assure you my friends will step up to the plate when needed. What else is troubling you?"

"Nothing more. Just some things for you to think about before we go any further."

"Then there's something I want you to think about. Life is cheap in Miami, Mr. Stavros. One person disappears, another pops up to take their place." He paused a beat. "Sometimes, their seat at the table remains empty. I'd bear that in mind if I were you."

"Duly noted." He stood. "If you're serious about partnering up, I'll be around. If not, I'll stake out my own claim." He raised his palm. "Praise the Lord."

"What happened?" Felicia asked when they were away from the club.

"I think I got to him. I could tell by his reactions. He'll check out Vargas, and he may look at Salazar in a different light, too."

"I've been thinkin' about that," Bones said. "Maybe we can goose the action by makin' Turk think that Salazar came over to our side."

"That would drive a wedge between them, but how do we do it?" Nick asked.

"Haven't figured that part out yet."

They proceeded toward their car, but Nick abruptly stopped and looked around the parking lot as something came to him, something he noticed before but didn't think was important until then.

"What is it?" Felicia asked.

"Something's out of place. Turk's car isn't in its reserved spot and Salazar isn't inside."

"So?" Felicia quizzed.

Nick looked at her. "Neither is Jimmie's girl, Jalisa. The women we saw the other night were scattered around the club, but she isn't here. When I asked Turk where Salazar was, he said he was running an errand."

"You don't suppose Salazar took her someplace, do you?" McCoy asked.

"Remember the threat Turk made to get Jimmie to play along?" Nick replied, then addressed Felicia. "Where is his GPS tracker showing the car?"

Felicia consulted her phone. "Collins Avenue and 92nd Street, near Surfside."

Nick's mind raced. "That's the budget end of the strip. Lots of mom-and-pop motels and cheap bars. We need to get over there."

They got into the car, and McCoy sped out of the parking lot, narrowly avoiding a fender bender with a Mercedes. He weaved in and out of traffic, ignoring the speed limit and the traffic lights that turned red as he raced through.

"What do we do when we get there?" he asked. "If Jalisa went with Salazar on her own, he could have us arrested."

"Don't bother me with details," Nick answered.

They cruised north along Collins Avenue until they found the intersection they were looking for. Felicia consulted the GPS on her phone.

"Comin' up on it," she said. "About a quarter mile on your right."

McCoy slowed as they reached the Silver Pelican Motel. He pulled into the parking lot, came to a stop, and turned off the headlights. The place was on the cheap side, with a faded blue and yellow neon sign and a smaller red one announcing they had vacancies. The lights flickered as though deciding whether to stay lit or give it up.

Nick scanned the nearly vacant lot, homing in on Turk's car. "Over there, on the right."

McCoy pulled into a space further away. After a few minutes, they saw a young black man, dressed in drooping jeans and a tropical shirt, approaching room twelve. He carried what appeared to be a large bottle in a brown paper bag and knocked on the door. When the door opened, the sound of loud music with a funky street beat poured forth.

"If that's not a party, I'll buy you a bar in Jamaica," Felicia said.

"Make sure it's on the beach," Nick said.

"What now?" McCoy asked.

"We need to see if the girl's inside, but we're probably under-equipped," Nick answered.

McCoy shut off the engine. "Not necessarily. I had a feelin' we'd need supplies, so I brought some."

They got out of the car, and McCoy popped open the trunk. Nick looked at the Ruger assault rifles and flash grenades. "Man, you came prepared."

"Never leave home without 'em. How do you want to play this?"

Nick handed one of the guns to Felicia, then took one for himself. "Blitz attack."

They approached the door and took positions on either side. McCoy readied a flash grenade and gave Nick a quick nod. Nick pounded on the door with his fist. When it opened a crack, McCoy threw his weight against it, tossing the grenade inside. All three of them shielded their eyes as the grenade exploded, bringing cries of surprise and loud cursing from inside. They charged into the room.

Salazar stood near one of the beds, coughing violently and

rubbing his eyes. Four other men were in the room. Through the haze, Nick saw Jalisa lying on the other bed, but she wasn't moving.

Nick charged at Salazar, but the Spaniard regained enough of his senses to take a wide swing. Nick ducked, swung the butt of his rifle upward, connected with Salazar's chin and sent him backward onto the empty bed. He sprang to his feet and charged at Nick with his fists doubled up. Before he could get a fight started, Felicia brought the barrel of her gun down hard on the back of Salazar's neck, sending him to his knees with an anguished cry of pain. She followed up with a swift kick to his jaw, one that dazed him and ended with the gun pressed against Salazar's temple.

"Don't," she ordered. "And get your hands behind your head."

Salazar took deep breaths while lacing his fingers together on the back of his neck and giving Nick a mean-eyed glare, one that communicated more than words. Nick bound Salazar's hands behind his back with a zip tie. He patted him down, removing his gun and a small bag of pills from his pocket.

Meanwhile, McCoy had four men lined up against the wall under gunpoint. One of them had stripped down and held his boxer shorts in front of him.

"Any weapons or drugs in your pockets, get 'em on the table," McCoy barked. "Now!"

The three who were still dressed complied, resulting in two switchblades, a box cutter, and a .25 caliber automatic pistol, along with several joints and two small bags of white powder.

"What's going on here?" Nick demanded.

"Hey, man, we just havin' a little fun, ya know?" the man in boxers answered.

"Who's throwing this party?"

"My man Antonio," he said. "Told us he got a fine piece for

rent and did we wanna party a little. What are you—some damn Kojak?"

"Yeah. Who loves ya, baby?" He addressed McCoy. "Get them outta here."

The man with the boxers bent to pick up his clothes, but Nick trained his gun on him. "Nobody said you could get dressed."

"Come on, man," he pleaded. "I can't go out like this."

"I don't see anything worth covering up. Haul ass!"

While McCoy herded the men from the room, Nick and Felicia went to Jalisa. He felt her pulse while Felicia checked her eyes.

"She's really out of it."

"Her pulse is weak, too," Nick added.

"Rohipnol?" Felicia asked.

Nick saw the empty wine glass and bottle of Chardonnay on the nightstand. "Looks like it." He went to Salazar and nudged him with the gun barrel. "On your feet."

"I had a feeling about you," Salazar sneered as he stood. "You a Fed?"

"Just a guy who doesn't like to lose. Get outside."

They left the room, and Nick guided Salazar to their car. He told McCoy to open the trunk, then ordered Salazar to climb in. When he was secured, Nick and Felicia went back to the room. Nick yanked the comforter from the other bed and draped it over Jalisa. Felicia picked up Jalisa's handbag and checked the room for any other personal items. Nick scooped her up, carried her to the back seat of the car, sat her upright, and buckled her in.

"Now what?" Felicia asked.

"We'll drop you and Jalisa off at the condo so she can sleep it off," Nick replied. "When she wakes up, get plenty of fluids into her, especially juice, and don't let her leave. Take her cell phone, too." He handed her the bag of pills he had taken from

Salazar. "Hide these someplace. I may need them."

"What are you gonna do with Salazar?"

"Take him to a little hideaway where no one will find him."

CHAPTER TEN

About three miles offshore from Key Largo, on the Atlantic side of the island, sat a Coast Guard watchtower built on concrete and steel pilings, fifty feet tall. It commanded a view of the ocean and the surrounding uninhabited keys. On a clear night and with a powerful telescope, one could see everything within a two-mile radius. The interior was a small apartment, with a bedroom, bath, kitchenette, and common room, complete with a water supply and a generator. The former lighthouse, dated to the 1880s, was deeded to the Coast Guard years earlier to stem the flow of refugees trying to make their way to America.

The lookout post had been closed for several years, a victim of the last recession and the government's ever-changing stance on immigration. Since then, it had ostensibly remained the property of the Coast Guard or the Department of the Interior, depending on which newspaper you believed. Neither agency seemed willing to spring for the upkeep.

Nick stood on the outdoor observation deck, gazing into the moonlit night while puffing a cigarette. All of the windows were covered by steel hurricane shutters. The speedboat they had used to get there was moored to one of the pilings, with a dark cover over it. He sipped his coffee while he checked his watch.

5:45. The sun will be creeping over the horizon in another hour. Sure is peaceful this time of night, before the daytime creatures rise from their slumber for another day of hell-raising. Sometimes I wish we lived on a deserted island somewhere.

Bones joined him, taking a drink from a bottle of water. "How did you find this place?"

"Through a fishing buddy in the Coast Guard. He brought me out here once."

"If this is government property, won't we get in trouble bein' here?"

"I wouldn't worry. According to my friend, the only time this place gets checked is if a patrol boat sees signs of life or they're on the lookout for illegals trying to get into the country."

"Seriously?"

"A couple of years ago they found ten of them hiding out here, thinking they'd reached the promised land."

"Isn't this technically in American waters?"

"A federal judge didn't think so. He ruled that it didn't meet the wet foot, dry foot policy and ordered all of them to be repatriated."

They went inside. The dank, stuffy room had a saltwater and mildew smell. Nick looked at Salazar, asleep on a cot, snoring with his mouth open and drooling.

"How much Ativan did you give him?" Nick asked.

"Enough to knock out a great white. He'll be out of it for another few hours."

Nick retrieved Salazar's cell phone when it lit up, reading the screen. "Turk's going nuts. This is the twelfth text he's sent telling Salazar to report."

"How does this help us?"

"It's the second string of the idea you had last night, about making him think Salazar switched sides. That's why I had you take a few pics of us together when we were getting into the boat to come out here."

McCoy nodded. "With what we did the other day, settin' up an offshore account in his name usin' Turk's money, that'll make him think he's a traitor."

"Exactly."

"When did you hatch this scheme without sayin' anything?"

Nick looked at him for a moment. "Not until last night when we raided that motel room. It was a serendipitous decision, and I seized the moment."

McCoy laughed. "I love it. How long are we gonna keep him on ice?"

"Until we get what we need. When he wakes up, we'll go to work on him. I just hope Felicia and the girl will be okay since Turk knows where we're staying."

"I took care of that. I assigned two operatives to the building, twelve-hour shifts around the clock. They're armed."

"Good men?"

"Former Army Rangers. They'll be safe."

Nick took Salazar's wallet from his hip pocket and examined the contents. He removed a thick stack of money.

McCoy let out a low whistle. "Man, look at all that green. Must be a few hundred there."

"Most of it in used tens and twenties. How much do you suppose he was charging those homeys for their turn with Jalisa last night?" He flung the wallet to the floor in disgust. "Pig."

Nick took Salazar's cell phone to the other side of the room. Sitting on a folding chair, he scrolled through the saved text messages.

"Anything?" McCoy asked.

Nick focused on the screen. "Here's one he sent to Vargas, telling him to check me out."

"Shows collusion. What else?"

Nick scrolled through the text messages without finding anything particularly interesting, until he typed Vargas's name into the search app. His eyes narrowed when he read one of the messages.

"Here's one from two months ago. Salazar told Vargas to locate Jasmine Blake and find out where she was working."

"The girl Brillstein told you about, the acid attack victim?"

"Uh-huh." Nick read the response. "Vargas told him which club she was working the night she was attacked. Son of a bitch used the cops to do his grunt work."

Nick switched to the calendar. "Salazar's calendar lists weekly appointments for Turk's clubs, his thrift store, a pawn shop in Little Havana, and an indoor arcade in Coconut Grove."

"Pawn shops and arcades are primarily cash businesses. You think that's how Turk's laundering his money?"

"It's making more sense. Salazar probably takes the money Turk makes from his escorts and dealers, then runs it through those places. Very tidy."

"Good if we want to sic the IRS on him, but how does it help us?"

"Since we're trying to make Turk think Salazar went into business for himself, this makes it look more credible. He picks up the take at the clubs and puts it through the wash after helping himself."

"What about his contacts?"

Nick tapped the appropriate app to scroll through the names in the address book. "Lots of numbers and e-mail addresses, but most of them only use initials, no first or last names. It would take us a long time to run all of these down."

"I'll forward it to the office and have one of my tech geeks work on it. Any photos?"

Nick tapped the gallery app. His gaze locked onto three stored photos showing him when he visited Bahama Joe's the first time. He held it out for McCoy to see.

"What do you want to bet he forwarded these to Vargas so he could ID me?"

McCoy shook his head. "Sucker bet. I'll pass. Anything

else?"

Nick looked through the rest of the photos but stopped when he found a series of shots showing a distinguished-looking older man making out with one of the young women from the bar. Nick laughed as he showed it to McCoy.

"Recognize him?"

McCoy looked at the images. "Vaguely. Who is he?"

"The guy who does the sports on one of the Miami TV stations."

McCoy nodded. "Oh, yeah. Doesn't he host an annual telethon for disabled kids?"

"Uh-huh. This would take his public credibility down a notch. I wonder what Turk's getting out of him to keep quiet about this?" He set the phone down. "See if you can disable the GPS, will ya?"

Nick stepped out to the observation deck to call Felicia's cell. She answered on the second ring.

"Hey, it's me," Nick said. "How's everything?"

"She's still asleep but comin' out of it. Where are you?"

"It's better if you don't know for now, but I'm okay." He hesitated. "I miss you."

Her voice softened a bit. "I miss you, too. I wish you were here. Every time I hear a noise, I pull my gun."

"You'll be okay. Bones posted a couple of armed guards in the building. Just keep the curtains closed and don't answer the door."

"What do I do when she wakes up?"

"See if you can get her to talk, find out what you can. If she was hanging around Turk's club, she must know something."

"How long are you gonna be gone?"

"Long enough to rattle Turk's cage. Call me later?"

"You got it."

Salazar slept when Nick went back inside. McCoy sat next

to a packing crate. He held up a deck of cards. "Play a little Gin?" he asked.

"Make it five-card draw and you've got a deal."

"I'm a little short at the moment."

Nick picked up Salazar's wallet and removed the cash. Pulling up a chair, he divided the money evenly between them.

"Deal 'em."

Bones shuffled the deck and dealt five cards. Nick arranged his in the correct order, then tossed a bill into the pot. "Open for ten."

Bones matched. Setting his cards face down, he picked up the deck. "How many?"

Nick set two cards off to the side. "Two."

Bones gave him his replacement cards. "Dealer takes three."

They played out their hand, raising and calling until the pot had grown. Nick laid his cards face up on the crate.

"Full house, kings over eights."

Bones tossed his cards down. "Beats two pair."

He shuffled the cards, dealt another hand, then made an opening wager. "Why did you really take this gig?" he asked.

"You mean why did I stick my neck out for something that doesn't involve national security or the preservation of mankind as we know it?"

"Yeah. If there was a big payday, I could understand, but what're you gettin' out of this?"

Nick looked at his cards and discarded two of them. "Satisfaction, maybe a little validation."

Bones dealt two cards, then took two for himself. "Do you really need reassurances that you've still got what it takes to get the job done?"

"Not really, but it's nice to know I can still beat the bad guys when I have to. Why did you come along for the ride since there wasn't a payoff?"

McCoy examined his cards, then placed a twenty in the pot. "Maybe for the same reason. I'll level with you, man. I have a great gig, runnin' that security company. Billion-dollar corporations have me on speed dial, and I prob'ly turn down more social invitations in a week than most people get in a month."

Nick matched his bet. "Sounds cushy compared to being a field agent."

"That's the problem. It's too cushy. Sometimes I feel like I'm goin' soft. I don't get many opportunities to work outside of the office." He paused. "After what I saw in that motel room last night, I knew I had to see this thing through."

"You've still got your heart in the right place."

"That ain't the only reason I'm doin' this."

Nick looked curiously at him. "Something you'd like to share?"

McCoy looked into his eyes. "I had a cousin named Rochelle, a coupla years older than me. We grew up together in South Philly. We were pretty tight." He glanced down and grinned in remembrance. "Man, I thought she was the coolest person ever. Honor Society, head cheerleader, total knockout, had guys fallin' all over themselves to get her attention, but she always found time for me, ya know? She was always helpin' me with my homework and lettin' me hang out with her and her friends. I really looked up to her."

Nick sat back in his chair. "What happened to her?"

McCoy took a deep breath. "All that popularity caught up with her. She got mixed up with the wrong crowd and met a guy sorta like Turk Morgan. His street name was Bennie Juice. He was the go-to for anything you wanted in my neighborhood."

"Bennie Juice?"

McCoy shrugged. "It was the nineties, man. Everyone was

still into the street hustle and Superfly thing. Anyway, he got her into the parties, clubs, drug scene, all that shit. Ruined her future. She even had a full ride to Penn State." He hesitated and cast his gaze down. "When she got into that lifestyle, we lost touch, and the last time I saw her was at the funeral. OD'ed on a hot shot."

Nick gave him a moment. "What happened then?"

McCoy slowly raised his gaze to meet Nick's. "The Juice got squeezed. Don't ask me anything beyond that."

Nick slowly nodded, casually displaying his cards, not asking any more questions. "I hate to do this to you, but I've got a straight flush."

Bones threw down his cards in disgust. "Damn! I forgot you never lose at poker."

Nick raked in his winnings. "So here we are, a couple of gunslingers past our prime, trying to prove we can still put one foot in front of the other without falling on our faces. Some life."

"Beats the alternative."

Felicia sat in a chair with her legs tucked under her, sipping a cup of herbal tea. Stray beams of sunlight filtered in through the partially opened curtains, giving way to a new day.

Jalisa, in a fitful sleep, murmured softly, and her legs kicked at the sheet. Her long, braided hair was disheveled and carelessly hung around her face and over the t-shirt Felicia had slipped on her. While getting her ready to sleep off her unintentional hangover, Felicia looked at the tattoos on Jalisa's upper arms, one depicting a teddy bear, another an angel.

Jalisa's clothing wasn't torn. She didn't have any bruises, abrasions, or scratches on her legs or torso, either.

Looks like we got there before anything got started. Thank God.

Jalisa slowly awoke and looked around through half-opened eyes, blinking a few times. Her gaze locked onto Felicia, and she suddenly came awake. She sat upright, pushing back against the headboard and pulled the sheet over her.

"Who are you?" she demanded.

Felicia responded in a soothing tone. "My name's Felicia. I'm a friend."

Jalisa gave her a suspicious gaze. "Friend of whose?"

"Yours, if you'll let me." She hesitated. "And I'm a friend of Jimmie Rae."

Jalisa's look and voice softened a bit. "Jimmie. Ain't thought about him for a while."

"He's been thinkin' about you."

Jalisa closed her eyes and rubbed her temples. "Where am I?"

"Someplace safe."

Jalisa eyed her for a moment. "I've seen you before. You were at Bahama Joe's the other night."

"That's right. Do you remember what happened last night?"

She slowly exhaled. "I remember bein' at the club, then goin' to some place in Surfside."

Felicia handed her a glass of orange juice from the nightstand. "Drink some of this."

"What is it?"

"Just juice. You need the sugar."

Jalisa took a small sip, then drained the glass. "Can I have some more?"

Felicia refilled her glass, and Jalisa drank it down. Drawing her knees toward her torso, elbows on her knees, she handed the glass to Felicia. Her face rested in her palms. "My head's killin' me."

Felicia shook two aspirin from a bottle and handed them to her with a glass of water. After Jalisa took the pills, she slid down into the bed on her side, curled up in the fetal position.

"What else do you remember?" Felicia gently prodded.

"Turk said there were some guys he wanted me to meet. Said they could help me with my career."

"What career?"

"I'm a singer. I didn't want to go, but he said it would do me good. Salazar took me to this motel, but there wasn't anyone there." She paused. "He poured me a glass of wine. Said it would loosen me up, get me relaxed for my big audition."

Felicia gave her a few moments. "Then what happened?"

"It's all a blur. I remember feelin' dizzy and lyin' down on the bed. I musta passed out 'cause that's all I remember."

Felicia took a deep breath to get her pulse and anger under control. "You said you're a singer. Is that how you got mixed up with Turk Morgan?"

"Mm-hmm. He heard me singin' back-up for a band one night and said he could get me into somethin' better."

"Did he?"

"Not yet. Keeps tellin' me I need more practice, but all he has me do is hang around his club on South Beach." She paused. "You said you're a friend of Jimmie's?"

"Yeah."

"How is he?"

"He's worried about you."

"Why?"

"Prob'ly because he cares about you."

Jalisa gave a small smile. "He's a special guy, but he shouldn't waste his time worryin' about me."

"Why not?"

"'Cause I did him wrong. We got each other through rehab, but I walked out on him."

Felicia shifted in her seat, then sipped her tea. "You weren't happy?"

"He started makin' a name for himself with his music.

Guess I wanted the same thing. I shoulda stayed with him instead of gettin' sucked in by Turk Morgan."

Felicia had a thought. "Did he do that for any other girls, promise to make them stars?"

"A few. We all hang around his place waitin' for our big break. We even joke about it, call ourselves the Pussy Posse."

"Does he expect all of you to entertain his friends?"

Jalisa stared at her. "A few of 'em spread their legs for his buddies. He says if they don't party with his friends, he won't help 'em get to the big time. It's all a con."

"So why did you stick around?"

Jalisa thought for a few moments. "Maybe I thought I'd be the one, you know, the one lucky enough to get my time in the spotlight for who I am, not for somethin' I had to do to get there. How long I got to stay here?"

"Just a little while, until you're straight."

She yawned and closed her eyes. Felicia watched her drift back to sleep, then walked to the window. She looked out at the emerging sun shining off the calm ocean waters, highlighting a few early morning swimmers and beach joggers. She was startled by Jalisa's soft drowsy voice.

"You think Jimmie would take me back?"

"Yeah, I do."

She continued gazing at the scenery while processing everything Jalisa had told her. *We've got to take this guy down.*

CHAPTER ELEVEN

Nick stood on the observation deck, listening to Felicia recount Jalisa's story over the phone. His heart pounded, and his blood pressure rose the longer he listened.

"Son of a bitch doesn't take no for an answer, does he?" he said.

"Doesn't sound like it. If he orders Salazar to commit date rape to keep his girls in line, what else is he capable of?"

"Ask Jasmine Blake. What I don't understand is if Jimmie told Turk he'd play along, why would he single out Jalisa for the treatment?"

"Maybe he didn't tell him yet, or he got stubborn."

"That would be just like him to mess up a good plan by growing a backbone when I told him to stay out of it."

"Speakin' of plans, what's yours?"

"We're gonna convince Turk that his people have turned on him. I put a question in his mind about Vargas last night, and he's going nuts trying to locate Salazar. It's time to turn up the heat."

"I got an idea about that. I checked Turk's website. Later this morning, he's makin' an appearance at a church to raise money for one of his so-called charities. If his main bodyguard is MIA, he might get rattled if you show up."

"He might at that. Good thinking, angel, and text me the address. Will you be okay staying there with Jalisa?"

"Yeah. She's not in any shape to travel, and after what happened last night, I think she's too scared to go home."

"Okay. Do you need anything?"

"Just you."

"I'm working on it."

He disconnected. Back inside, he poured the last of the coffee he'd picked up before they left the mainland.

"What's goin' on?" Bones asked.

Nick spent the next few minutes relating what Felicia had told him.

Bones slowly shook his head in amazement. "Turk sounds like those human traffickers we used to come across in Central and South America, the ones who preyed on girls from the poor villages."

"A pimp by any other name . . ."

"What now?"

Nick glanced at Salazar, who was coming out of his sleep. "Time to convince our houseguest that Turk has written him off. After that, I'm going to that fundraiser where he's appearing."

"How do we make Turk think he's all alone?"

"We start by showing him those pics I had you take last night."

Bones accessed the photos on his phone. He scrolled through them while Nick looked over his shoulder. He had staged them to hide Salazar's hands bound behind his back. Nick had his arm around Salazar's shoulder and was smiling while talking to him as they walked along the pier where the boat was moored. He pointed at one shot.

"That one. Send it to my phone."

Bones punched in Nick's cell number. "Done."

Nick slipped off his jacket and tossed it aside, leaving his shoulder holster and gun on prominent display. He opened a bottle of water. Dashing some of it in Salazar's face, he woke him up, sputtering and coughing. He looked around in confusion, attempted to sit up, but his feet were bound at the ankles along with his hands behind his back. Nick stepped over to him, pulled him upright, and leaned him against the wall.

"Where the hell am I?" Salazar demanded while struggling against the bindings.

"In a faraway land where no one will think to look for you," Nick replied. He took a flask from his jacket pocket, removed the cap and held it near Salazar's mouth. "Drink this."

Salazar shook his head. "You poisoned it."

Nick laughed. "Give me some credit, Salazar. If I'd wanted you dead, we'd be having this conversation through Madame LaZonga and her crystal ball. Go on, take a sip. It'll clear your head."

He hesitated before he took a small sip of the scotch whiskey the flask contained. Nick put the flask back in his coat pocket, pulled up a chair, and sat. Bones stood nearby with his arms crossed over his chest.

"You think you can get away with puttin' the snatch on me?" Salazar taunted. "When Turk finds out what you did, ain't no place you can hide."

Nick looked at Bones. "He talks a good game, doesn't he?"

"Yeah, but deep down, he's really a pussycat."

"Emphasis on pussy," Nick added, then addressed Salazar. "Time for you to face a few facts. You've been off the radar for twelve hours. You weren't there to tuck your boss into bed last night. He probably thinks you bailed on him and took a better offer."

"What better offer?"

Nick looked at him for a moment. "The one for you to come work for me."

Salazar scoffed. "You crazy, gringo. Turk knows I'd never throw in with someone else."

"He's paying you that much?"

"Loyalty's worth more than money."

Nick was about to respond when a thought hit him. *He's*

right. What did Turk do to buy Salazar's loyalty? "That's very noble. In my experience, a lot of hoods wouldn't feel that way. It's sort of an old school concept, sticking together for the good of the outfit. Unless you owe him big time for something that's pretty important to you."

Salazar cast his gaze down but remained silent. Small beads of sweat appeared on his bald head.

"You're a two-time loser with a long rap sheet," Nick said. "Your last assault conviction should've sent you away for twelve years, but you got out in two. Did Turk arrange that, so you'd owe him?"

Salazar remained silent, but his breathing got heavier.

"Or perhaps he got to one of your family members." He hesitated. "Maybe you have a sister that caught his eye, one he just couldn't keep his hands off of. Maybe he threatened to put her to work on the streets if you didn't throw in with him."

Salazar raised his head and gave Nick a killer look accompanied by a hard-set jaw and angry tone. "You leave my *familia* out of this, or I swear, I'll rip your fucking heart out and shove it down your throat."

Bingo. I found his sore spot. "Is that what happened?"

Salazar closed his eyes for a few moments. "Her name's Sophia. When Turk saw her, she was only nineteen." He looked Nick in the eye. "Nineteen, man. Not old enough to know what it took to get along in the world, but young enough to get turned on by some bling and a few dollars."

"Turk took advantage of it?"

"Yeah, he took advantage. It's what The Man does best. I told him to lay off, and he said if I put in with him, he'd leave her alone."

"So, you joined his organization."

"What else could I do? He took care of me. When I got jammed up on that prison thing, he called in some favors to get me an early parole. After that, I didn't own my soul anymore."

"Where's your sister?"

"I sent her back to Madrid where she belongs. This world up here, it ain't safe for us big folks, let alone a kid." He smirked. "Helluva country you got here, gringo. You tell ev'ryone to send their poor and their needy, but when the chips are down, it's tough tamales. Helluva country, this United States."

"Don't judge it by one greedy asshole. That thing you were doing last night. Is that how he keeps the women who work for him in line?"

Salazar hesitated. "Usually the ones who bitch about workin' in his clubs or on the streets in Overtown. Sometimes it's the ones that owe him money and don't wanna work it off."

"Why pick Jalisa?"

"Turk said he wanted to send a message."

Nick's brow furrowed. "A message to whom?"

"He didn't say."

"What does he really want?"

Salazar stared at him for a few moments. "Power. It's all about power and control with him. Control over me, over you, the girls, hell, the whole damn world."

Nick stood, motioning for Bones to join him in the next room.

"What do you think?" Nick asked in a low voice.

"He sounds sincere, but it could be an act. I'd want to check out his story, see if he really has a sister in Spain."

"Can you do that?"

"Shouldn't be too hard. What're you gonna do in the meantime?"

"Pay Turk a visit."

CHAPTER TWELVE

The courtyard behind Our Lady of Hope church in Liberty City was occupied by about fifty people, all ages, listening in rapt silence as Turk Morgan spoke from the steps. The hibiscus bushes and cypress trees were in full bloom, adding some color contrast to the well-hydrated, neatly trimmed lawn. A mild breeze blew in, offsetting the late morning heat.

Nick stood on the fringe of the crowd, listening to Turk extolling the work the church performed for those in need and encouraging the good brothers and sisters to open their wallets rather than their hearts. He also made a pitch for his planned Funk music museum, reminding the masses to visit his website and donate whatever they could spare, promising it would be a boost to the local economy. Nick studied the faces in the crowd. Many seemed to be mesmerized by every word Turk spoke.

He really knows how to work a crowd. This looks like a zombie convention.

When Turk concluded, he gave his customary *Praise the Lord* sign-off, which elicited an enthusiastic *Amen!* from the crowd. Turk made his way to the refreshment table, stopping to shake hands and pose for pictures. Nick tagged the man he had seen at Bahama Joe's the night before, the one he called Rico, standing nearby but not close enough to get his picture taken.

Nick waited until he had gotten a glass of champagne, then casually approached the table, grabbing a glass of bubbly for himself. Turk caught sight of him and nearly choked on his drink. Nick offered a polite smile.

"Nice speech. It should shake loose a few bucks."

Turk gave him a narrowed look. "This is a fundraising event for the poor black and Latino citizens who live in the ghetto, Mr. Stavros."

Nick sipped his champagne. "I made a generous contribution when they passed the hat. They didn't seem to mind my ethnic origin. I guess my green overshadowed my white."

"Point taken. What are you really doing here?"

"Research. I know this is part of your laundering operation, and I wanted to see it for myself."

"You seem to know a lot about my business affairs. I'm not sure I like that."

"I think you're missing the point. I'm just an ordinary thief, and I know all about you and your business. Think what someone could find out if they were really trying."

"You're referring to the authorities or perhaps the Internal Revenue Service?"

"To mention a couple, yes. You've left yourself wide open."

Turk finished his champagne in one swallow. "Someone as clever as yourself must know a portion of my profits manages to find its way into the right pockets."

"If that doesn't work, I'm sure you have other methods of persuasion."

"Meaning what?"

"Blackmail comes to mind."

Turk's face scrunched in confusion. "Blackmail. Such an ugly word, one I'm not familiar with."

Nick chuckled. "I'm sure you keep all those pretty young women in your club just to improve the décor."

"I don't know who you've been talking to, but it appears someone has given you some erroneous information about me. If I knew who was spreading such slander, I'd consider suing them."

Nick looked around the immediate area. "Where's your number one boy, Salazar? Still running errands?"

Turk's gaze narrowed, and his face tightened. "Mr. Stavros, I've had just about enough of you."

"You won't do anything about it, though, at least not here."

"I might remind you that I can play this game as well as you. Perhaps better, since you're on my home turf. For the good of all concerned, I'd suggest that our paths not cross again."

He turned to walk away while taking his phone from his pocket. Nick let him get a few steps before he called out to him.

"Hey, Turk, if you're trying to reach Salazar, he's no longer taking your calls."

He slowly turned to face him. "What are you talking about?"

Nick took his phone from his breast pocket, accessed the photo McCoy had forwarded and held it up.

"Looks like he accepted a better offer," Nick said. "See you around."

He left before Turk could respond. Behind the wheel of the car, he waited for Turk and his bodyguard to leave and followed at a safe distance. They took the route to South Beach and an hour later had parked outside Bahama Joe's. Nick pulled into a parking space around the corner and shut off the engine, not really having a plan. He answered his phone when he recognized McCoy's number.

"I heard back from one of my intel people," Bones said. "Salazar's story checks. He has a younger sister named Sophia, and she's livin' in Madrid. According to customs, she was in the States until five years ago on a visitor's visa but went back home before it expired."

"Looks like he was telling the truth. Anything else?"

"Yeah. You'd better haul ass out of there and grab Felicia on the way."

"Why?"

"That wire you planted in Turk's club. He was just on the phone with Vargas, readin' him the riot act for not keepin' tabs on you. He gave him orders to find you and Salazar ASAP. That means he'll go to the first place he knows to look, and that's the condo. I already alerted my people, but if he shows up with a warrant, they won't be able to stop him."

Nick looked at his watch. "I'll save him the trouble. How's Salazar?"

"Asleep. I freshened up his Ativan cocktail."

"Man, I hope you never get mad at me. If he says anything else noteworthy, call me."

Nick drove to the condo, weaving in and out of traffic. He pulled into the gated parking lot and walked up the steps. When he reached the entrance, he saw Vargas pull to the curb half a block away, driving the sports car Nick had rented, with the top down. Nick peered around the corner and watched. Vargas remained seated, looking at the building through a pair of aviators.

He isn't coming in, so I'm guessing he doesn't have a warrant, and he's driving his own car. What's his game plan?

Nick walked across the marble lobby to the elevator but slowed when he spotted a man sitting in a lounge chair off to the side. He was solidly built, with crewcut hair, dressed in a tropical shirt and khaki slacks, pretending to read a magazine. Nick stopped and looked at him. The man peered at him over the top of the magazine for a few moments. Nick gave a quick nod, going on his way. He arrived on the sixth floor and knocked on the door.

Felicia's eye looked through the peephole before she opened the door to give him a firm hug followed by a kiss. "You didn't tell me you were comin' over."

"I didn't know it myself until a few minutes ago. Are you okay?"

"Yeah, just a little tired."

"How's the patient?"

"Still sleepin' it off. What's goin' on?"

"New game plan. We're making Turk think Salazar came to work for me."

"How are you doin' that?"

"We took away his cell so he can't reply to any of Turk's texts, we already funneled money into a dummy account in his name, and McCoy took some shots of me acting chummy with Salazar. I sprung it on Turk when I went to that fundraiser you told me about."

"You think he bought it?"

Nick shrugged. "We'll see. Bones called to tell me that Turk was on that bug I planted, ordering Vargas to track me down. That's why I came over. He's parked out front."

"Vargas is outside right now, lookin' for you?"

"Yeah, and he's going to find me."

Felicia clutched his arm, her eyes communicating her fear. "Hon, if you let him take you in, I'll never see you again."

"He's not taking me anywhere. I need that stash of roofies we took from Salazar last night."

Felicia went to the kitchen and returned with the small plastic bag. Nick took out his handkerchief and used it to place the baggie in his outer jacket pocket.

"I need you to call Vargas's precinct and ask to speak with someone in internal affairs. Tell them Vargas tried to sell you drugs at the Edison Hotel bar last night, but you turned him down. When he put the moves on you, you told him to stop. He flashed his badge and said if you didn't sleep with him, he'd bust you for possession. Tell them he's been stalking you all day, he's sitting outside your building right now, and you're afraid he's going to attack you when you go out. Make sure you describe the sports car he's driving. Got all that?"

Felicia laughed softly. "Yeah."

"Really sell it."

While Felicia placed the call, Nick went to the bedroom and peeked in on the sleeping Jalisa. He recalled everything Felicia had told him and compared it to Salazar's story.

Man, I've run across some sleazy hoods in my time, but Turk's in a class by himself.

He went back to the living room and listened with amusement to Felicia's impassioned complaint.

"How was I?" she asked after disconnecting.

"You're ready for Broadway. Think they bought it?"

"If they didn't, they're as corrupt as Vargas. They said they'd send someone over. What about Salazar?"

"He's out of circulation for the moment."

"You gonna let him go?"

"No. Turk's on the run. After the conversation I just had with him, I could tell he's getting worried. We'll need Salazar to seal the deal. Are you okay with Jalisa staying here?"

"We'll be all right as long as McCoy's men stay awake."

Nick handed her a slip of paper. "That's the cell number for the guy pulling duty downstairs. Call him if there's any trouble."

"What should I tell Jalisa if she asks questions?"

"Enough to put her at ease but not too much and keep her away from any phones. We don't need her calling Jimmie or anyone else right now."

"Nick, shouldn't we report this to the police? Jalisa was taken to that motel to be sexually assaulted. Even if she was drugged, that's still attempted rape."

He ran his hand along her arm to her hand. "I know it was but look at the evidence. Even though she didn't know she was being drugged, the defense would make it out like she was a willing party girl. You said you didn't find any physical trauma when you put her to bed, and she can't recall much about what happened. They'd also bring up her past drug history and the fact she went there voluntarily. It might be more humiliating for her to go through that, and the charges would never stick."

Felicia thought for a few moments. "I suppose you're right. I just don't like not seein' her get justice for this."

"She will." He checked his watch. "I'd better get downstairs."

"What're you gonna do with those pills?"

"Use them to get Vargas out of the way."

Felicia took his hands, pulled him close, and planted her lips firmly on his. Nick folded her in his arms and kissed her while enjoying her scent. Felicia's tongue darted into his mouth, and he kissed her with more passion.

He pulled back and caressed her cheek with his palm. "I should go."

"I know."

She kissed him again, running her hands along his shoulders. "You really should go."

"I know."

"Why don't you?"

"I can't."

She gave him one more kiss, then stepped back. "Go before I take you prisoner."

Nick sighed. "If you insist. I'll call you later."

He took the elevator to the lobby. The man in the chair was still in position, reading the same magazine. Nick exited the building and stood on the top step, looking at Vargas around the corner of the building. He reached into his pocket to ball the small bag of pills in his right hand then let his hand hang at his side. He strolled to Vargas's car.

"Detective Vargas. To what do I owe the pleasure?"

"I've been looking for you, Stavros."

Nick rested his right hip and arm against the driver's side, dropping the baggie of pills behind the seat while maintaining eye contact with Vargas. "Congratulations. You found me. That was some fine detective work, waiting outside my building until I showed up. Do you treat all of your cases with such finesse?"

"That's cute. I'm taking you in."

Nick stepped back, gazed the length of the car, and let out a low whistle. "This is the sexiest squad car I've ever seen. I didn't realize the Miami Beach police had such an extravagant budget."

"Never mind the wisecracks. This is my personal vehicle."

"You must pull a lot of overtime, or is Turk paying you that much to be his errand boy?"

Vargas's eyes narrowed. "You watch your mouth, mister."

"Forgive me. Did I step too close? Does errand boy rub you the wrong way? How about gopher or flunky? Do those do anything for you?"

"Stavros, I'm gonna enjoy giving you some of that famous third degree you've heard about when I claim you resisted arrest."

"We both know if I get in that car, I'm not going to headquarters."

"Maybe not right off. Someone wants to see you first. Then maybe I'll take in what's left of you."

"On what charge?"

"I don't need one. You're on the Interpol list as a person of interest." He laughed. "Hell, with your record, I may walk away from this with a commendation from the Mayor or the director of the FBI. I can see the headline now — *Local Detective Captures International Criminal.* They may pin a medal on me."

Nick glanced to his right when he heard two cars rapidly approaching, followed by squealing tires and brakes. One was a black sedan and the other a patrol car with a police emblem on the doors. "Maybe sooner than you think."

Two men in suits exited the unmarked car and approached, followed by two uniformed officers. One of the suited men was tall and fit, with sandy brown hair and a neatly trimmed mustache.

"Detective Vargas?" he asked.

"Yeah. Who are you, and what the hell do you want?"

The man flashed his badge. "Captain Doug Boren, Internal Affairs. We've had a complaint about you. You need to come with us."

Vargas smirked. "Piss off. I'm on the job, working a case."

"According to your squad commander, this is your day off. What are you doing here?"

"This guy is a person of interest in an ongoing criminal investigation. I was about to take him in."

Boren looked at Nick. "Do you have some ID?"

Nick took out his wallet and showed him his fake driver's license, hoping that Boren wouldn't examine it too closely.

"It's about time you guys got here," Nick said.

Boren handed him his wallet. "What do you mean?"

"I came home from a business trip, and the first thing my girlfriend hits me with is a story about some vice cop who tried to sell her some drugs last night at the Edison. He even threatened to run her in if she didn't sleep with him. She said he's been following her all day, and she saw him outside our building."

"You came down here to confront him?"

"What would you have done, captain?"

Boren gave a wry knowing smile. "Probably the same thing. Is your girlfriend the one who called us?"

"Yeah, but she didn't want to. She was afraid of what this guy might do."

"That's bullshit," Vargas angrily asserted. "This man has a criminal record."

"And your personnel file is oh-so-clean," Boren inter-rupted. "This isn't the first complaint we've had about you, Vargas. We're going to have a nice long talk about it at head-quarters. Maybe you'll tell us how a vice cop can afford a fancy car like this. Step out of the vehicle."

Vargas gave a disgusted exhale, got out, and assumed the frisk position, with his hands on the hood and his legs spread. Boren patted him down and took his gun while one of the uniformed officers searched his car.

"Captain Boren," he said.

Boren turned to look at the officer holding up the plastic bag of pills Nick had planted. Boren took a pair of cuffs from his belt and pinned Vargas's hands behind his back.

"Detective Vargas, you're under arrest," he said. "I suggest you keep your mouth shut until you talk to your lawyer and your union rep."

Nick watched them herd Vargas into the squad car.

A wise man once said that a smart person always knows his lim-itations. I guess Vargas missed that lecture at the police academy.

CHAPTER THIRTEEN

Felicia stood in the kitchen, putting the finishing touches on the food she had prepared. Jalisa had wakened and wanted to take a shower

I know we should've taken her to the ER or reported her assault to the cops, but it would've been hard to prove anything without evidence. We don't really know how many people Turk has in his pocket, either. I just hope she can come to grips with this over time.

Jalisa emerged from the bedroom and perched on one of the bar stools at the counter. She had on one of Felicia's polo shirts and a pair of slacks.

"Feel better?" Felicia asked.

"A little. My head still feels like I'm in a vacuum."

"It'll pass."

"Thanks for lettin' me borrow your clothes. I'll wash them before I give them back."

"No rush." She placed a plate in front of her. "I thought you might be hungry."

"Thanks. What is it?"

"Tuna salad. It's a recipe I learned from my mom."

She took a small amount on a fork. "This is good. Where are you from? Jamaica? The Bahamas?"

"Close. Barbados."

"Never been there. Never been anywhere outside of Florida."

Felicia sat next to her with her own plate. "Maybe you'll get to some of those places one day."

Jalisa smirked. "Only in my dreams."

Felicia watched her attack the food like she hadn't eaten in a week and asked, "It's been that kind of life?"

Jalisa took a long drink of water. "One nightmare to the next. Guess that's why I got suckered by someone like Turk. Thought he was my ticket out of hell."

Felicia nibbled at the food on her plate. After their conversation earlier that morning, she had decided to keep the conversation as upbeat as possible. "Do you come from a big family?"

"An older brother who was in and out of jail, a younger sister, a mother on disability, and an absentee father. There wasn't much to go around, but we made it."

"Sounds rough."

"I don't like to talk about it."

"I understand."

"I heard you talkin' to a man earlier. Who was it?"

"Nick. He's my boyfriend." She grinned. "I guess I should say significant other because that's what he calls me."

"Is he a cop?"

"No, but he's one of the good guys. He wants to help you, too."

Jalisa looked puzzled. "Why are you doin' all this for someone like me?"

"You mean why are we doin' this for a stranger?"

"Yeah. I'm nobody to you. Why waste your time on a poor piece of ghetto trash like me?"

"You're not trash, Jalisa. You're a person. Stop thinkin' of yourself like that." She paused to get the conversation on a more positive track. "Tell me about Jimmie. What kind of life did you two have before you split?"

Jalisa gave a small smile. "It was pretty good. We met in rehab when we were both takin' the big cure. We made a pact that we'd keep each other clean."

"You were good together?"

She nodded. "I called him my Jimmie Bear." She pulled up her sleeve to show her teddy bear tattoo. "That's why I got this tat."

"Looks just like him."

Jalisa giggled. "What about your life with this Nick fella? Pretty good?"

A smile overtook her face. "Yeah, it's pretty damn good. He's a great guy."

"What makes him a great guy?"

"Lots of things. I suppose the main thing is that he cares."

"About what?"

"The important things, like people and doin' the right thing when he sees things that aren't right."

"Sounds like a nice guy. Where did you find someone like him?"

Felicia hesitated, not wanting to reveal things from the past. "We kind of found each other. Guess it was fate, sort of like you and Jimmie. You gonna go back to him?"

Jalisa pushed her empty plate aside and stared at the counter. "I don't know if I can. How many?"

"How many what?"

"How many guys were there when you found me in that motel room last night?"

"Does it really matter?"

"It does to me."

She considered her answer for a few seconds before responding. "Four, but we got there before anything happened."

Jalisa shifted in her seat. "I hate that bastard Turk. I want to see him and Salazar suffer."

"We're workin' on it."

She put their plates in the sink, refilled Jalisa's water, and poured herself a cup of coffee before taking her seat.

"You were the middle kid in your family?"

"Yeah. I was like a black Jan Brady."

Felicia laughed. "That's pretty good."

"What about you? Do you come from a big family?"

"Yeah, and I'm the oldest. Sorry about that."

"What are you sorry about?"

"That I can't relate to what you went through," Felicia told her sincerely.

"Were you there when your brothers and sisters were growin' up?"

"Yeah, we were always close."

Jalisa looked down. "At least they had someone like you around."

Felicia sipped her coffee. "Sounds like you could've used a big sister to talk things over with."

"It woulda been nice to have someone I could talk to about stuff."

"If the job's still open, would I qualify?"

Jalisa looked at her with unexpected fiery eyes. "Seriously? Look, I'm grateful to you and your boyfriend for gettin' me outta there last night and givin' me a place to dry out, but I'm too old for this social worker routine. I don't need you or anyone else wastin' your time on me."

"That's the third time you've said that."

"Said what?"

"Wastin' time on you. Where the hell is that comin' from?"

Jalisa didn't answer but cast her eyes down. Felicia decided to take a hard approach. She put her fingers under Jalisa's chin and forced their eyes to meet.

"I know you didn't grow up in the best environment and you're tryin' to make up for it, but if you wanna get someplace in this big bad world, lose the street attitude. You think you're not worth worryin' about? Think again. There's a lot of people who care about you. Your family, Jimmie, me, Nick, and a strange guy you've never met named McCoy. You gotta stop thinkin' that you're a nobody."

"I just never had anyone who cared about me before."

"That's my point. You've never had that, and it's why someone like Turk Morgan was able to take advantage of you. His radar sensed that you were vulnerable, so he brought you into the fold. Start havin' some respect for yourself, and you'll get respect from everyone else."

"Are you saying this was my fault?"

"No, it wasn't your fault, but you've got to start believin' in yourself, Jalisa. Nobody's gonna hand you a career. You have to work for it. That's the only way you get somethin' worthwhile out of this miserable thing called life."

Jalisa was silent for a few minutes. Tears formed in the corners of her eyes. "I guess if you wanna play big sister, that wouldn't be so bad."

Felicia grinned. "I'd rather be your friend."

"I'd like that, too."

Nick coasted the boat to the dock beneath the observation tower. After securing it to the dock cleat, he pulled out the plastic bag with supplies he had picked up and threw the black tarp over the boat. The rickety elevator to the observation deck creaked and moaned on its journey. Nick hoped it wouldn't die along the way.

He entered the room and saw Salazar sleeping on the cot. He also saw a strange man sitting nearby, watching Salazar. The man, well-muscled with light brown crewcut hair, had a holstered gun on his belt, and a marine tattoo on his upper arm. He gave Nick an unsmiling glance, then resumed his watching.

Nick walked over to McCoy. "Friend of yours?"

"I figured we could use some re-enforcements, so I had him brought out here."

"You do remember that we're not getting paid for this, right?"

"Yeah, we are. When we tapped Turk's bank accounts, I took out enough to cover expenses."

Nick laughed. "Way to go. Does he have a name?"

"You can call him Jack."

He handed Bones a sandwich from the sack. "I brought you some lunch."

"Thanks. I'm starvin'." He unwrapped the sandwich and removed the top piece of bread. "You got me corned beef on rye, but you forgot the mustard?"

"There's just no pleasing you, is there? Anything new from the wire?"

McCoy took a bite and chewed before he answered. "Turk's in a panic. He's callin' in a lot of favors to find you, Salazar, and the girl. He can't get hold of Vargas, either. What happened to him?"

Nick sat, unwrapped his turkey bacon club and took a bite. "I arranged for internal affairs to pick him up."

"How'd you manage that?"

"I went to the condo after you called, and he showed up like we thought he would. I had Felicia call his precinct and tell them he tried to sell her drugs and was stalking her all day. I planted the drugs we took from Salazar in his car. The IA guys found them and took him into custody."

Bones laughed. "Beautiful. How's the girl holdin' up?"

"She was still asleep. Something Salazar said about last night has been bugging me. He said Turk wanted to send someone a message."

"What about it?"

"Was he trying to make a point with Jalisa that she needed to put out for his buddies or was it intended as a message for Jimmie Rae?"

"You think he's been holdin' out on you?"

"I think that's pretty extreme just to get Jimmie to change talent agents. Brillstein said Turk targeted his headliners, the ones with a big following. That could be why he wants Jimmie, but Jalisa said she's been a back-up singer and never had a solo career. Why would he try so hard to get her to come over to his side?

Bones took a long swallow of bottled water. "Maybe Jimmie knows somethin' about Turk, and he's usin' her as leverage to buy his silence. Salazar said that's how he operates."

"Could be."

"Now we've got him lookin' over his shoulder, but how do we put him out of business?"

Nick finished his sandwich. "When the internal affairs cops picked up Vargas, they grilled him about the sports car and found the drugs I planted. Vargas will likely rat Turk out to get himself a better deal."

"That may jumpstart an investigation, but it could take time. I've been thinkin' about a different angle. He's proud of his public image as a do-gooder, a Robin Hood for the folks in the poor neighborhoods. What if we found a way to turn those people against him?"

"How?"

"Social media. Everybody has a cell phone. We could plant some items on the net about how he really makes his money and what he does with the donations he gets."

Nick nodded. "That might work. If enough people read it, Turk's political contacts would run for cover."

"What about this Jimmie Rae thing? You gonna ask him about it?"

"Yeah. I just need to figure out a tactful way to tell him his girlfriend was almost an unwilling party girl."

"Why not level with him, make him see how serious this really is?"

Nick shook his head. "If I tell him what Turk did, Jimmie

will go after him again, and I won't be able to talk him out of it."

"Can't say I'd blame him, but you're right."

"In the meantime, let's convince Turk that he's all alone. We took Vargas out of the way, and I made him think Salazar may have joined the other team."

"What do you have in mind?"

"How do you suppose he'd react to someone trying to kill him?"

CHAPTER FOURTEEN

Felicia sat in the living room, watching TV with the sound turned down low. She glanced over at Jalisa napping on the couch. *Poor kid. Thought she saw a way out of the low-rent area and look what happened. Prob'ly had visions of a mansion on Star Island and singing to a sell-out crowd of fans. I hope Nick's plan works. Turk deserves to be put six feet under.*

Her gaze snapped to the door when she heard a series of knocks. *Who the hell could that be?*

She quietly approached the door and looked through the peephole, seeing a young black man holding a pizza box and wearing a red-and-white striped shirt emblazoned with the logo of a local pizzeria.

"Who is it?" she asked.

"Pizza delivery, ma'am."

I didn't order a pizza, and if Nick did, he would've told me. "Just a minute."

She hurried to the bedroom, took her Beretta nine-millimeter pistol from her purse and jacked the slide on top, forcing a bullet into the chamber. She went back to the living room and draped a comforter over Jalisa, covering her completely. She unlocked the door, then flattened herself against the wall, her gun at the ready.

"Come on in."

The door slowly opened, and the young man entered, looking around the room. He stopped when his gaze focused on the couch. He took a pistol from the waistband under his shirt and leveled it at his target.

Felicia pressed the barrel of her gun at the base of his skull. He gasped.

"If you squeeze that trigger, I'll blow your freakin' head off."

The man stood motionless. Felicia took his gun, tossed it aside, then pressed hers against his temple. She patted him down, removed his wallet and stepped back, keeping her gun pointed at him. She flipped open his wallet and verified his face against the one on his driver's license.

"Put the box on the table—slow—and get your hands in the air."

He did as she ordered.

"Who sent you here?"

"DeMarco's Pizza. You called for take-out."

She quickly glanced at the order ticket. "Nice try, but the name on the ticket is yours." She aimed her gun at his head. "Is that your final answer?"

Small beads of sweat appeared on his upper lip. "Look, lady, I'm just followin' orders. The boss says go, and I go."

Felicia's internal rage simmered. She locked onto his gaze and held it while speaking in a low intense tone.

"You made a delivery to the wrong address. Do you know how easy it would be for me to shoot you and claim you forced your way in? Maybe that's how they do things in your neighborhood, but you try that shit up here, you get your ass shot off. You go back to your boss and tell him he's screwin' with the wrong gang. Got that?"

The man licked his lips. "Yeah, I got it."

"Good. There's just one more thing."

She pulled her arm back and quickly brought the barrel of her gun into contact with his face, cutting his cheek.

The man cried out in surprise. He recovered from the shock, then wiped the blood from his face with his palm. "You crazy bitch! What'd you do that for?"

"Just makin' sure you understand." She tossed him the wallet. "Get outta here."

He made a fast exit. Felicia secured the door, grabbed her cell phone, and punched in the number Nick had given her earlier.

"This is unit 612. There's a guy comin' downstairs, young, black, wearin' a red-and-white striped shirt with a gash on his face. He's one of Turk Morgan's flunkies. Check him out."

"Copy that," the man replied. "Everything secure up there?"

"Yeah but stay awake. These guys are playin' hardball."

Felicia disconnected and looked over at Jalisa, who was still asleep. Felicia opened the pizza box.

Pepperoni, mushrooms, and green olives with extra cheese. How did they know what I like?

She removed a slice, biting into it while walking back to her chair.

Nick sipped his iced tea at a table inside the 44th Street Diner in South Beach. He glanced at his watch. He had arrived early for his meeting.

Old habit. I always showed up early if I could. If someone said meet me at 10:30, I was there by 10:20. I seem to recall that I learned that lesson from my dad. He was probably the best contract negotiator General Motors ever had, and he always made a point of showing up early for meetings. He said it threw the opposition off balance, walking in and seeing him sitting at the table, ready to go to work while they were still pouring coffee and picking out donuts. That bit of wisdom served me well when I got into the spy game, making the other side wonder what I was up to. I'm glad I got out of that racket.

He looked up when Jimmie Rae slid into the booth across from him.

"Got your message," he said. "So whassup?"

His voice was listless, and his words were slightly slurred.

Nick sat back and looked at him for a moment. Jimmie looked tired and haggard, his bloodshot, watery eyes darting from left to right.

"Are you back on the pipe?" he asked.

Jimmie was aghast. "No, man. I told you I quit that shit. Why you askin' me that?"

"Because your lips say no, but your eyes say maybe."

Jimmie glanced down and let out a deep breath. "Ain't slept the last coupla nights. I've been callin' Jalisa, but she won't pick up. I'm worried about her."

Nick took a moment to compose his response. "Jalisa isn't answering because we took her out of the game. She's all right."

"Why did you take her out?"

"It was getting too dangerous, and I was afraid she'd get caught in the crossfire."

"Where is she?"

"She's with Felicia, and she's safe. That's all you need to know for now."

"So why the meet?"

"Just touching base. Did you call Turk and tell him you'd work for him?"

Jimmie paused for a few seconds. "No, I didn't."

Nick crossed his arms over his chest. "Why not?"

"Because I just can't get mixed up with that thief again. I told you that."

"Jimmie, there's something you're not telling me, and it's time to put your cards on the table."

"Why do you think I'm holdin' out on you?"

"Because the more I dig into this, the more things I find that don't make sense. Turk Morgan is a bastard who goes after what he wants and does whatever it takes to get it. You're a small fish, and he only wants the big game. Why is he so intent on having you sewn up in his pocket?"

Jimmie stared at the table for a few moments before answering in a subdued voice. "That stuff I told you about Turk was true, all those things when I was growin' up. He helped me and my family when we needed it, and he expected a lot in return." He smirked. "The Robin Hood of the ghetto, my ass. More like Robbing Hood. Give to the poor, then take it back times ten."

"That still doesn't explain his sudden interest in you."

Jimmie raised his gaze and looked at Nick for a few moments. "Ten years ago, I saw him kill one of his girls. He found out she was holdin' out, had her hooks into some politician who was payin' her more than the going rate. Turk confronted her and decided to make an example for the rest of his stable."

"What did he do?"

Jimmie hesitated. "He took her into an alley, beat the shit out of her and strangled her to death with his bare hands."

"Fill in the blanks for me," Nick interrupted. "Was anyone else there?"

Jimmie shook his head. "Just him."

"He let you watch him commit a murder?"

Jimmie paused. "He didn't know I was there until it was over. I was takin' a shortcut through that alley on my way home. When I saw what he was doin', I hid around the corner." He shook his head. "I couldn't believe it. I never saw anyone get killed before. It was like he was just totally outta control."

"How old were you?"

"Sixteen. He didn't know I was there until he was leavin'. Do you know what he did when he saw me? He put his hand on my shoulder and said that's what happens to people who don't appreciate his generosity. He told me I should remember that. Then he just walked away, all cool, as if nothin' happened."

"Why didn't you go to the cops?"

He gave a short, sarcastic laugh. "Turk would've loved that. I still had a mom and a younger sister livin' in that neighborhood, and he'd have taken it out on them."

"You said before that your family wasn't here any longer. Where are they?"

"Mom passed away a few years ago, and my sis lives in New York with her husband."

"You've kept your mouth shut for ten years. Why is he suddenly worried that you'll break your silence?"

"You read about his newest project, didn't you?"

"You mean that Funk music museum he promised to build but hasn't yet?"

"Yeah. He's lined up some big corporate money and a lotta entertainers to support it. He's pullin' in donations hand over fist and can't afford any bad press right now."

Nick gave a knowing nod. "He's afraid if you sign a big recording deal and leave Miami, he won't be able to keep you quiet. It would've been nice to know all of this before now."

"Okay, I shoulda told you. I didn't think this whole thing would get so complicated."

"Just what did you expect me to do?"

"I figured you could scare Turk off, get him to leave me and Jalisa alone."

Nick slowly shook his head. "Man, you must've heard some wild stories about my reputation. Did you know the woman he killed?"

"Yeah, I knew her from around."

Nick took a notepad and pen from his coat pocket and slid them across the table. "Write down her name, along with when and where it happened."

Jimmie did as he requested. "What are you gonna do?"

"See if I can use it against him since there's no statute of limitations on murder." He drank some iced tea. "I'm curious about this museum he has planned. According to the news archives, he promised to build it three years ago, but he hasn't broken ground yet. Why the delay?"

"Still linin' up workin' capital, or so he says. It's just another scam to separate the suckers from their nickels and dimes."

"How does he work it?"

"He talks it up at his public appearances and fundraisers, gets ev'rybody all excited, telling them to visit his website. He has a donation button on there, and it's linked to a collection service."

"People fall for his line of bull?"

Jimmie nodded. "Cash or credit, as long as they pay up. None of that bread finds its way to where he says it's goin', though. He works his charities the same way. He collects a lotta money, gives out enough to make it look legit and pockets the rest."

"Why doesn't someone call him on the delay for that museum?"

"Turk's a smooth talker, and he knows how to blow smoke up someone's ass. Whenever anyone questions him about it, he tells 'em what they wanna hear so they'll shut up. What do I do now?"

"Disappear. Find someplace to hole up where Turk's people won't find you. Just don't go home or back to your old neighborhood. That's the first place they'll look."

Nick took a burner phone from his pocket and slid it across the table.

"Use that instead of your cell. He may have people tracking your phone. My number's programmed into it."

"When can I talk to Jalisa?"

"Soon. I'll call you."

Nick watched Jimmie leave. *Crazy-ass kid. Why didn't he tell me this sooner? If he had, we could've had this whole thing wrapped up.*

He answered his cell phone when he recognized Felicia's number.

"Hon, somethin' happened," she began. "Turk sent one of his men over here disguised as a pizza delivery guy."

Nick's pulse sped up. "Are you okay?"

"Yeah, I took care of it. I called McCoy's man in the lobby, and he grabbed him before he could leave."

He exhaled a slow breath. "Do you still think that's the safest place for you two?"

"Yeah, as long as the watchdogs stay awake. Where are you?"

"Not far from you. I met with Jimmie to get a few answers."

"Like what?"

"Like why Turk's so hot to get him under his thumb. Jimmie witnessed him killing one of his hookers ten years ago. That has to be why he's doing this because he's afraid Jimmie will use it against him."

"He'd lose some of his precious control. Can we use it?"

"I think so, but first, I'm going to make a counterstrike. Where's Turk now?"

Felicia waited a few moments before responding. "Accordin' to the GPS, he's in downtown Miami. What're you gonna do?"

"Pay a visit to his club. I'll call you later."

Nick hurried to his car. A few minutes later he was parked across from Bahama Joe's. He quickly went inside. For late in the afternoon, the business was light, with only a dozen people occupying seats. He approached the bar and saw the bartender, a heavy-set black man, quickly reaching for something under the counter.

Nick pulled his gun and aimed it. "I wouldn't grab that piece if I were you. Step back."

The man scowled but did what he was told. "You must be

crazy, comin' in here and drawin' down on me."

"Yeah, that's what they call me, Crazy Nick Stavros. I'm so unstable I might shoot someone just for the hell of it. I haven't pulled the trigger in over a week, and I'm having withdrawal, so don't give me an excuse. Is the boss around?"

"Not until later."

"Be sure to tell him I stopped by and hand me a bottle of 151 but do it slowly."

The bartender retrieved a bottle of 151-proof rum and set it on the bar. Nick grabbed it, then went to Turk's private area. He poured the rum over the table, saturating the tablecloth and tossed the empty bottle aside. He took his lighter from his pocket, lit the edge of the cloth, jumping back as it burst into flame.

Nick quickly left the club as the fire alarm sounded and the sprinkler system kicked in. He pushed his way through the fleeing customers jamming the doorway. He went to his car where he watched as the fire department responded to the alarm.

Maybe that'll teach you not to send your flunkies after me and my loved ones.

CHAPTER FIFTEEN

"I can't believe you went after Turk on your own!" McCoy exploded. "You know what that means? He'll turn over every rock in Miami lookin' for you, and you put Felicia and the girl in his crosshairs."

"Then tell your bodyguards to be more alert," Nick fired back.

Bones pointed his finger. "That's a cheap shot, Nick. They can't brace everyone who walks into that building. How was my man supposed to know that a pizza delivery guy was really a gunsel?"

Nick calmed down. "He couldn't have, and you're right. When Felicia told me what happened, I lost control for a minute."

"Lost control, my ass. Sounds like you had a major meltdown. You used to keep it together better than that. What happened to you?"

"I rejoined the human race."

They stood on the observation deck while Jack stayed inside with Salazar. Nick gazed into the early evening sky, still clear with a slight breeze blowing in. A sailboat headed for shore and a cruise ship steamed south on the horizon. A flock of seagulls lazily flapped their way across the darkening horizon.

"Did your guy get anything from the man Turk sent over there?"

"Just name, rank, and serial number."

Nick handed him the note with the name Jimmie had provided. "The day wasn't a total bust. Jimmie Rae may have given us the bullet we need."

McCoy read the note. "Lashonda James. Who is she?"

"A woman Turk killed ten years ago, one of his call girls. Jimmie witnessed the whole thing. I think that's why he's trying to get Jimmie under his control, so he won't talk."

"Why wait until now? If he wanted to shut Jimmie's mouth, he coulda done it before."

"Remember that Funk music museum he's developing? It's high profile, and he can't have anyone doing anything to jeopardize it. When Turk heard about the recording deal Brillstein arranged, he didn't want Jimmie out of his reach. That's why he coaxed Jalisa into his corner, to use her so Jimmie would keep his mouth shut. Salazar said he wanted to send someone a message, and that was it."

"I get it. He's a control freak, and he wants everyone to mind their manners. I'll have someone check out this name. What are we gonna do about Turk?"

"We're gonna lay low for a while and let him stew about what's happened. He lost Vargas and Salazar, his ambush at the condo was a bust, and I showed him I'm not afraid to confront him on his home turf."

"You want to force him into makin' a play?"

"Yeah. He can't maintain that cool façade of his forever. He's gonna crack."

His disposable cell phone rang. "Maybe he already has." Taking it from his pocket, he held it up for McCoy to see. "Turk's private number." He put it on speaker. "Yeah?"

"Mr. Stavros, you made a grave error today," Turk said in a voice laced with anger. "You shouldn't have made such a stupid play in one of my establishments. I don't like what you did."

"I didn't do it for your amusement. While we're on the subject, I don't like you sending cheap gunmen after me."

There was a hesitation of several seconds. "Point taken. It's time we had a talk."

"Weren't you the one who said you'd had quite enough of me?"

"My feelings haven't changed, but I now realize you're someone who should be taken seriously."

"Are you suggesting a truce?"

"I'm willing to discuss a compromise."

"I'll get back to you."

He disconnected before Turk could answer. "What do you think?"

"I think he's afraid you'll show up at his house and start another fire."

"Good. If he's paranoid, he's vulnerable."

"You gonna meet with him?"

"Let him sweat. In the meantime, get a couple of your people to start that negative online vibe you mentioned. Now that we know what's really important to him, we can attack it."

Felicia sat with Jalisa in the living room that evening, sort of watching TV. It was on, but Felicia wasn't really paying attention to the action on the screen. Her mind kept drifting to what had happened over the previous few days.

I know I had some doubts about us gettin' involved in this, and the deeper we dig, the more I don't like what's goin' on. This is a whole netherworld, an underground that people don't hear about. When you read those tourists brochures and travel ads, they only show the bright lights and beaches, not the other parts of the city, like where Jalisa and Jimmie grew up. Prob'ly wouldn't sell too many plane tickets if they showed some of those neighborhoods.

She was brought back to reality. Jalisa laughed at something from the TV in a young giggly laugh, like that of a teen-ager getting a kick out of something some silly sit-com character had done.

"Did you see that?" she asked. "He's so funny!"

"I wasn't payin' attention."

Jalisa used the remote to turn down the volume. "What's wrong with you? You've been quiet all night."

"Just thinkin'."

"About what?"

Felicia hesitated. "About how I wish Nick was here."

Jalisa cast her gaze down. "Yeah, I've been thinkin' about Jimmie, too. You really miss this Nick fella?"

"He's nice to cuddle up with at night. He makes me feel warm and safe. You miss Jimmie like that?"

Jalisa nodded. "More than I knew. Guess it took all this to make me realize that."

"I have a feelin' you two will get back together when this is all over."

Jalisa looked at her. "When what's all over?"

Felicia hesitated. *She doesn't know what this is all about, but maybe she should.*

"I'm gonna fix some tea. Would you like some?"

"Never been a tea drinker. Wouldn't know what kind to ask for."

Felicia stood. "Chamomile. It helps you sleep. Sound okay?"

Jalisa covered her mouth when she yawned. "I don't think I'll need it but okay."

Felicia went to the kitchen to heat the water in the micro-wave and returned a few minutes later with two cups of tea. She set them on the glass-topped coffee table, then sat cross-legged on the floor. She indicated a spot on the other side of the table, and Jalisa joined her.

"Is this something you used to do with your brothers and sisters?" she asked.

"Didn't you ever sit around a campfire when you were a kid?"

"We didn't have too many of those in Liberty City unless someone's house caught fire."

"Guess I didn't think about that." She sipped her tea. "Jalisa, you need to know what this is all about and how you got dragged into it."

"You mean why I'm here?"

"That's part of it, but there's somethin' I want you to understand. Nick and I don't live here. He owns a club in Key Largo, and that's where we live. Jimmie plays at our place, and he's a big hit down there."

Jalisa smiled. "I always knew my Jimmie Bear would find his crowd."

Felicia took another sip. "He did, and that's a big part of this. He has a good gig comin' up next month at a club on the Beach. His agent—"

"Brillstein?"

"That's the guy. Brillstein called in a favor and lined up a record producer from LA to hear Jimmie. Could be the start of somethin' good."

"Wow," Jalisa softly uttered. "I always knew he'd make it."

"He still might, but Turk Morgan started puttin' pressure on him to ditch Brillstein and sign with him. Jimmie asked Nick to get Turk to leave him alone." She paused. "The real reason was because he wanted you to come back."

Jalisa gave her a curious look. "You mean you and your boyfriend took me out of Turk's world because Jimmie asked you to?"

"That's how it started, but when we found out more about Turk, we wanted to expose him for what he really is. Last night, after we went to Bahama Joe's, Nick noticed that you weren't there, and neither was Salazar. We tracked him to that motel where we found you, saw what was goin' on and brought you here."

Jalisa stared into her cup for a few moments. "Never had anyone pay so much positive attention to me before." She looked up, her eyes communicating a softness, an understanding Felicia hadn't detected before. "Thank you."

She stretched her hand to meet Jalisa's and gave it a firm squeeze. "You're welcome."

"Is this one of those big sis moments?"

Felicia laughed. "It's more like a BFF moment. Is that okay with you?"

Jalisa smiled. "Yeah, it's okay." She sipped her tea. "What you said about your life with this Nick guy. How did you know it was the right thing, that he was the one you wanted to be with?"

Felicia thought of a good response. It was tough for her to pinpoint an exact *Eureka* moment, there had been so many. Was it when they worked together in England or when they first kissed? Was it when Nick lost his wife and was emotionally adrift, like someone in a life raft waiting to be rescued? Was it the first time they made love?

"Prob'ly when I thought it was time for me to go back to Barbados, and he asked me to stay here."

"Did he propose?"

Felicia giggled. "More like an indecent proposal. Neither of us was lookin' to jump the broom."

"Why did you decide to stay?"

Felicia looked at her. "It just felt natural."

Jalisa nodded. "Think I can meet him someday?"

"He'd like that, but I should warn you, he can be kinda tough."

"Can't match me when it comes to bein' tough."

"I can believe that."

CHAPTER SIXTEEN

2:00 in the morning, the dead of night, the idle time when everything was calm for the moment while everyone regrouped and devised their next plan of attack. Nick was stretched out on a cot in the bedroom of the observation tower, his fingers laced behind his head, trying to relax after a busy day. His mind roamed to thoughts of Felicia, miles away, barricaded in a safe house with armed guards. Their brief visit earlier had only served to remind him how much he didn't like being away from her. He felt a warm internal glow as he thought about all of the fun times they'd had since she moved in with him.

Every day's a new adventure with her, a new day for discovery. She really brought me back to life when she became a part of my world.

As he drifted off to sleep, his subconscious mind brought forth the memory of when Felicia had first moved in with him, after they'd been reunited on a cold case from the CIA's archives a few years earlier.

Nick slowly emerged from his slumber, lingering in the half-awake early morning twilight where you can't quite tell what's real and what's a dream. The emerging sun filtering through the blinds revealed Felicia lying next to him, although with his arm wrapped around her and his body pressed against hers, he didn't need to see her to know she was there. She had been a comforting presence all night, one he hadn't experienced in far too long. He pulled himself tighter against her, burying his face against her neck, and inhaling her scent. He planted a kiss on her cheek, waking her.

Felicia's eyes slowly fluttered opened, and she rolled over, giving him a sleepy smile. She touched his cheek with her palm.

"Good morning," she softly said.

"Good morning, angel. Sleep well?"

"Mm-hmm. You?"

"Best night's sleep I've had in a long time."

"You're sweet. What're we gonna do today?"

He played with a strand of her long hair. "Explore."

"Explore what?"

"Everything I've been ignoring the last few years."

Felicia ran her fingers through his hair. "Why did you start callin' me angel?"

He peered into her soft sleepy eyes. "Maybe because you saved me."

"From what?"

He kissed her. "Myself."

Nick was jolted out of his reverie by a hand on his shoulder, shaking him.

"Nick, get up," Bones said in a low voice. "We got company."

Nick scrambled to his feet and grabbed his gun, following Bones outside. They crouched on the darkened observation deck, listening. Waves slapped against the pilings below, and Nick heard voices in the distance.

"Did you see anything?" he whispered.

"Yeah, a boat. I heard it comin' from the mainland. It stopped about fifty feet away, starboard side." He handed Nick a pair of binoculars. "Take a look."

Nick focused the binoculars equipped with night vision lenses and searched in the direction Bones indicated. The three-quarter moon was clear and provided enough light for Nick to make out a four-passenger jet boat containing three men, dressed in black, their complexions allowing them to blend in with the night. All of them had pistols in belt holsters. One of them picked up an assault rifle and handed it to one of the other men. They spoke amongst themselves.

"You think they're Turk's men or scavengers who saw us hangin' around out here?" Bones asked.

"Whoever they are, they mean business. They're all packing heavy heat. Maybe they're mules, waiting for a drug drop."

The men sat in the boat, rocking with the evening tides. Nick focused on their faces.

"I recognize two of those guys from Turk's club."

"How did they find us?" Bones wondered.

"Do you suppose Turk had someone track Salazar's cell through the GPS before you disabled it?"

"He might have. What now?"

Nick watched them. "Wait 'em out and see what they do."

Five minutes passed with no unusual activity. One of them stood at the side of the boat, unzipped his pants and took a leak, eliciting soft laughter from the other two. He resumed his seat, lit what appeared to be a cigarette and took a puff. He coughed a few times, then passed it to one of the other men, who repeated the ritual.

"Great," Bones said. "Hitmen with a buzz on. This should be fun."

"These guys are playing it way too cool," Nick commented. "They haven't launched an assault so I'm thinking one of two things — they're waiting for reinforcements or meeting someone."

Bones looked at the boat. "They haven't scoped us out yet, either. If they were gonna take us out and get Salazar, they would've made a move by now."

Nick's attention was captured by the sound of another craft approaching from the distance. He focused the binoculars on a yacht bearing north. The diesel engines subsided, and it coasted to a crawl, sidling up near the jet boat. One of the men caught the rope tossed to him, pulling the two boats closer.

"I'll be damned," Bones muttered. "Looks like you were right about a drug drop."

They watched as four plastic-wrapped parcels were transferred from the yacht to the other boat. Five minutes later the transaction was completed, and the yacht departed, heading north toward Miami. Nick expected the jet boat to leave but became confused when the three men stood and drew their sidearms. One of them took aim at the tower, fired a single shot, and hit the radio antenna atop the structure. He laughed, and a second man stepped up for his turn.

Nick and Bones flattened themselves on the deck.

"Seriously?" Bones asked in a low frenzied tone. "Target practice?"

"Do you have a gun with a night vision sight?"

Bones handed him one of the assault rifles. Nick got to his knees and rested the barrel on the railing. He braced the stock against his shoulder, adjusted the illuminated sight, and took careful aim at the man on the boat.

"You gonna pick 'em off?" Bones asked.

"Nope. Just scare the shit out of them."

He focused on the edge of the boat just in front of the man aiming at the tower. Nick waited until he heard the blast from the man's gun, then immediately squeezed the trigger, causing an echoing bang and splintering of the boat deck near his feet.

The man jumped back in surprise, nearly falling over one of the seats. Nick heard him exclaim. "Damn! What the fuck was that?"

Before one of them could fire back, Nick clicked a bullet into the chamber and let loose another shot that shattered half of the windshield. In a jumble of panic, the three men fell over one another, cursing loudly. Nick focused on the fuel hose at the rear of the boat. His next shot grazed it, sending a spout of fuel into the air.

"Get on your feet, drop your weapons, and get your hands in the air!" Bones called out.

One of them scrambled to the pilot's seat, but Nick fired another shot that ricocheted off the steering wheel. The men hurriedly tossed their guns aside, and their arms shot up into the air.

"Hey, man, don't kill us!" one of them yelled. "We're just doin' a little business out here!"

"Get into the water," Nick called.

They climbed overboard, treading water.

"Now what?" one of them yelled.

"Swim."

They all looked at each other but didn't make a move. Nick fired a shot directly in front of them. The men cried out in surprise, thrashing to swim toward shore. When they were in the distance, Nick and Bones sat with their backs against the railing and laughed. Bones extended his hand.

"Lucky Nick. Nice bluff."

"Thanks. Let's finish the job."

They went down to the dock, uncovered their boat and rode out to the jet boat. Nick climbed into the pilot seat and fired it up. He drove the boat into the Atlantic with Bones following him. When the severed fuel line began to sputter, he shut off the engine. Gathering up the four bundles the men had picked up, he took out his knife and made a small cut in one of them. He placed his wet fingertip into the white powder it contained, tasted it, and spit it out, recognizing the bitter taste of cocaine. He cut several slits in each bundle before he held them underwater until they sank. He climbed into the other boat, and Bones headed for the tower.

"If those guys make it back to shore, they'll tell Turk what happened," Bones said. "He'll figure you were responsible and send more troops this way."

"Yeah. We'll head out at daylight. Time to put this caper to bed. Do you have a place where we can stash Salazar?"

"Wouldn't be surprised. How're you gonna goose Turk into action?"

"I'll arrange to meet with him so we can discuss a deal."

The rising sun made a slow ascent, dissipating a light curtain of gray fog that hung over the ocean. Nick checked his watch. It was 8:00. He stood on the shore while Bones and Jack secured Salazar in the trunk of the car.

Taking out his disposable cell, he punched in Turk's number. "This is Stavros," he said. "I'm ready for a sit-down."

"Very good, Mr. Stavros. I'm certain we can come up with a mutually beneficial solution to our differences."

"You're boring me, Turk. Where and when?"

"I could see you this afternoon at four-thirty, at Club Masquerade."

"A public place. I like that. One ground rule, though—you only bring one bodyguard, and I'll do the same."

"That's a reasonable demand. I'll see you this afternoon."

Nick disconnected. *Like hell, you will.* He dialed Felicia's cell number.

"Hey, it's me. How are you two doing this morning?"

"Not bad, except for one thing."

"What?"

"I missed cuddling with you last night."

Nick grinned. "Must be contagious. I had the same problem."

He spent a few minutes recapping their late-night adventure, assuring Felicia that he was all right.

"What're you gonna do now?" she asked.

"We're moving to a safe house, and I've arranged to meet

Turk this afternoon so we can hammer out a deal."

"Hon, you can't meet up with him. He'll have his people ready to gun you down."

"You think I don't know that? I'll meet with him but not when he expects me. In the meantime, I need you and Jalisa to clear out of there. After what we did last night, Turk's going to send his people looking for me and that condo is where they'll start."

"Where should we go?"

"Take her to our place in Key Largo. Call a livery service. They use unmarked cars."

"Got it. When am I gonna see you?"

"Very soon, I promise. Call me if anything happens."

He put away his phone and climbed into the passenger seat.

"Everything good?" Bones asked.

"As good as it can be."

"Ya know, after what we did last night, Turk's gonna come after us with everything he's got. The only place he knows to look for you is the condo. That means Felicia and the girl are targets."

"He can't hit a target that isn't there. I just told Felicia to go to our place in Key Largo."

"She's takin' Jalisa with her?"

"Of course. I need you to leave your men in place, in case Turk sends more of his guns over there. They might get lucky and catch them breaking and entering."

Nick and Bones stood across the street from a high-rise office building on Flagler Street. Nick stared at the shiny glass structure through sunglasses while casually puffing a cigarette. The sidewalks were a maze of stylishly dressed office dwellers, all hurrying to get somewhere important, not bothering to notice the few panhandlers who begged for their attention.

"You sure Turk's here?" Bones asked.

"His GPS tracker says he is."

"Surprised he hasn't wondered why you keep showin' up wherever he happens to be."

"What did I say about him being cocky? He thinks no one would dare to track his whereabouts."

"Lucky for us he's arrogant."

"And careless."

"Aren't they one and the same?" Bones chuckled. "Man, he's gonna shit when he sees you."

"That's the idea, and it's why I set up our face to face meeting for later today. This way, he won't have time to plan an ambush."

"I figured that's what you had in mind."

"You know me too well."

He nudged Bones with his elbow when Turk Morgan and the man called Rico emerged from the building, accompanied by another man Nick didn't recognize. Turk wore one of his tailored gray suits and carried an expensive-looking, tan briefcase. He shook hands with the man and raised his palm before strolling toward the parking lot down the street.

Nick and Bones sprinted across the street to stand at the parking lot entrance.

Seeing him, Turk abruptly stopped for a moment before casually approaching. "Mr. Stavros," he said. "You have a knack for showing up at the most inopportune times."

Nick shrugged. "I was in the neighborhood."

Turk glanced at his gold Rolex. "Our meeting is set for four-thirty across town."

Nick gave a sly grin. "Is it?" He gestured at the briefcase. "Nice man-purse. Calfskin?"

Turk stared at him for a moment. "Ostrich. Business discussions are usually conducted with a certain amount of decorum and protocol. A parking lot doesn't meet that criteria."

"Neither does one of your nightclubs with your hired guns ready to ambush me when I walk in."

Turk paused for a few moments. "Fine, we'll talk." He glanced at Bones. "But in private."

"Sorry, but we're joined at the hip."

"I must confess that you have a larger network than I realized. My research indicated that most of your employees were in Europe."

"They wanted to visit Miami. I'm a generous boss."

"You and your people have caused some disruption to my operations. You try to steal my employees, vandalize one of my establishments, and interrupt my import business. I've also read some rather distressing comments made about me on the internet."

Nick looked aghast. "Who would do that to a nice guy like you? You're a pillar of the community and a friend to the downtrodden. If I were you, I'd demand a retraction."

"Enough games, Mr. Stavros. I'm a busy man, and I don't have time for you."

"I can understand that. It must be time-consuming, ripping off the poor, running drugs, arranging sexual assaults, things like that."

Turk's face tightened even more. "You're coming dangerously close to crossing the line. I have never been accused of doing anything remotely criminal."

"I suppose that's the beauty of having so many flunkies to do your grunt work." He paused for effect. "Speaking of which, have you spoken with your boy Salazar lately? He seems pretty happy with the package I offered him to come work for me."

Turk's gaze narrowed. "No, and one of my young lady companions also seems to have disappeared."

"Perhaps she traded you in for a younger man."

He exhaled a slow breath. "Let's cut to the chase, shall we? I said I was willing to discuss a compromise. What do you want?"

Nick pulled off his sunglasses and gave him a hard, penetrating stare. "Pick up your marbles and find a different playground."

Turk slowly shook his head while maintaining his intense stare. "Not going to happen."

Nick stared back at him. "Then don't say I didn't give you the opportunity to walk away with your ass intact." He raised his right palm. "Praise the Lord."

He and Bones crossed the street. Nick stopped when they reached the next intersection and looked back the way they had come. Turk's town car merged with the traffic going in the opposite direction.

"Man, if looks could kill . . ." Bones said.

"I'd be dead already," Nick finished.

They crossed the street when the light changed and entered the garage.

"Did you find anything on that name Jimmie gave me?" Nick asked, crawling into the passenger seat.

Bones took out his phone and accessed a page. "Lashonda James' family reported her missing ten years ago. She had a few misdemeanors for shoplifting and solicitation. The cops never came up with anything, including a body. It's still an open case."

"Maybe we can close it for them. If they didn't find a body, that means Turk had one of his goons dispose of her."

"Meaning?"

"Meaning there's another witness out there. You don't suppose good ol' Salazar did it, do you?"

"We couldn't get that lucky."

"Got an idea how we can turn up the heat. Have someone

post an item about the missing woman, something like *Whatever happened to Lashonda James?* List some of the stuff you uncovered, include her photo, and ask anyone with information to reply. See if you can drop Turk's name in there somewhere."

"What's that gonna accomplish?"

"He said he's aware of the other things your people have posted. If he sees that someone's asking questions about a murder he committed, it might work on his nerves."

"Worth a try. When's the big showdown?"

"Hopefully soon." Nick slowly wagged his head. "I'm getting tired of this. I want to get back to being a club owner and watching sunsets over the Gulf."

McCoy chuckled while starting the car. He put it in gear.

"What's so funny?" Nick asked.

"Never thought I'd see Nick Seven, the poster boy for a *bring 'em back dead or alive CIA spook* gettin' domesticated. You're losin' your touch, man."

Nick punched his arm. "Shut up."

"What was that you said the other day about provin' you still have what it takes?"

Nick looked at him. "You think I don't?"

He gave Nick a sideways glance. "You still got it. Feel better now?"

Nick settled into the plush leather seat and grinned. "Yeah. Thanks."

CHAPTER SEVENTEEN

The old mini-van slowed to a stop outside Nick and Felicia's condo complex in north Key Largo. The parking lot was mostly empty with the other residents gone to work or fishing for the day. Felicia and Jalisa exited the van and took out the two overnight bags. Felicia gave the Uber driver a tip, although, after an hour-long drive in a dilapidated van with no air conditioning and worn-out shocks that embraced every bump in the road, she wasn't sure why she bothered.

Felicia unlocked the door and then they went inside. While she disarmed the security system, Jalisa looked around the split-level dwelling in awe, taking in the Florida-themed furnishings and soft muted colors.

"Wow," she softly uttered. "You live here?"

"Uh-huh."

"Nice place."

Felicia went to the sliding glass door leading to the deck and drew open the drapes, flooding the room with sunlight. Jalisa approached the entertainment center and pointed at a framed photo of Nick and Felicia taken on the beach.

"Is this him?"

"Yeah, that's Nick."

Jalisa nodded her approval. "Not bad lookin', for a white guy."

Felicia laughed. "I'm glad you approve."

They went outside and sat at the glass-topped table. A gentle breeze blew in along the channel, billowing the sails of a

catamaran departing from a nearby dock. The deck was surrounded by coconut palm and banyan trees that swayed lazily. The aroma of grilled food from a restaurant further down
the channel wafted in, accompanied by Calypso music and
laughter.

"Your boyfriend must do all right," Jalisa commented.
"Guess maybe crime really does pay."

"What do you mean?"

Jalisa faced her. "I remembered where I heard his name before. Turk was talkin' about him after you two came to Bahama Joe's the other night. Said your boyfriend was some big-
time smuggler overseas."

Felicia paused, weighing how much information she
wanted to share. *If she thinks we're runnin' some kind of game,
maybe I should let her keep thinkin' it. On the other hand, not tellin'
her the truth might cause her not to trust me.*

"What if he isn't what you think he is?" she asked. "Would
that make a difference?"

Jalisa thought for a moment. "No, I guess not. You're
helpin' me, and I appreciate it. Is he a crook like Turk said?"

"Don't believe everything you hear. Let's leave it at that,
okay?"

Jalisa shrugged. "Okay. When I checked my purse before
we left, I couldn't find my cell phone. Have you seen it?"

"I have it."

"Why did you take it?"

Felicia looked at her for a moment. "For your own safety.
We didn't want you to call Jimmie and run the risk of Turk's
people findin' you."

"You didn't trust me?"

Felicia rested her hand on Jalisa's shoulder. "Only because
I didn't know you at first. I think you would've done the
same."

Jalisa grinned. "I guess I would've. You got street smarts.
Did you know that?"

"Thanks, I think."

"Where did you get 'em?"

"Around."

"I should let that go, too, huh?"

"For now."

Jalisa looked around, taking in the view. "Are we gonna be safe here?"

"Yeah. Turk doesn't know about this place."

"That's what you said in Miami."

"That was different. We weren't tryin' to hide from him up there."

Jalisa sat back and crossed her legs. "What're you and your boyfriend really up to?"

"I told you before."

"You wouldn't go to all this trouble just to get me and Jimmie back together. I've been around and I know a con game when I see one."

"Do you really want to know?"

"Weren't you the one who said we were friends? Friends tell each other what they want to know, so give it up."

Felicia laughed at her forthright attitude. "Okay, girlfriend, here goes. We started this because Jimmie asked us to, but we found out what Turk was really doin'. The cops won't touch him because he spreads his money around, so we decided to take him down."

"What's the payoff?"

"What do you mean?"

Jalisa gave an exasperated exhale. "Are you takin' over Turk's business or what?"

"No, we're just makin' sure he goes out of business."

Jalisa slowly shook her head. "You guys don't sound like any crooks I ever met up with. All of them were after somethin'."

"Disappointed?"

"Maybe a little. I still think you're holdin' out on me."

Felicia looked at her for a moment. "Do you trust me?"

She pondered her question. "Yeah, I trust you."

"Then bear with me. When the time's right, I'll tell you what it's all about. Deal?"

"Deal. Can I have my phone now?"

"Not just yet. It's . . ."

Jalisa held up her hand. "I know. It's for my own good."

"Why don't you just take it easy and think of this as a vacation?"

Jalisa smirked. "Vacations cost money and as long as I'm sittin' on my ass, I ain't makin' any. Did you think about that?"

Felicia gazed at the horizon for a few moments. "How much does Turk pay you to hang around his club lookin' pretty?"

"Enough to get by. What's it to you?"

"You said he expects you and the rest of the posse to entertain his friends and business connections. Did he ever suggest that you could make more money if you loosened up a little?"

Jalisa hesitated. "It was mentioned."

"You said no?"

Jalisa gave her a fiery look. "That's right, I said no. I never put out to get anything before and I'm sure as hell not gonna let someone pimp me out. Satisfied?"

"Yeah. You know somethin'?"

"What?"

"You've got street smarts, too."

McCoy pulled the car to a stop in the driveway of an older non-descript house in one of the less affluent parts of Homestead in south Miami. The yellow stucco needed a paint job, the old-style windows probably weren't the most energy efficient, and the fir tree in the front yard cried out for a pair of pruning shears. The late afternoon sun began its descent over the Gulf, casting shadows on the streets, accompanied by the sound of kids playing in the next block. He and Nick walked to the front door.

Salazar was tied to a chair in the nearly empty living room while Jack sat nearby. Salazar's hands were bound behind his back and his chin rested on his chest as he breathed evenly, asleep. McCoy lightly tapped Jack on his shoulder.

"Take a break and grab somethin' to eat. We'll take over for a while."

Jack stood, stretched, and left the room. Nick went to Salazar and raised his head to slap his cheek several times until he came around.

"Wake up," Nick said. "We need to talk."

Salazar blinked a few times to focus. He pulled against the bindings out of reflex, probably hoping they had been magically loosened. "How long you gonna keep me tied up like this?"

"Not much longer. Can you understand me?"

"Yeah, I hear you okay."

"Good. Now listen carefully. I'm going to mention a name, and you're going to tell me everything you know about the person. Are we connecting?"

Salazar eyed him warily. "If I don't?"

"Then I hope you can swim with your hands tied behind your back."

Salazar exhaled in disgust. "Fine. What name?"

"Lashonda James."

Small beads of sweat broke out on Salazar's bald head. "That was a long time ago, man."

"Ten years, to be exact. What do you know about her?"

"I know Turk told me to get rid of her body."

Nick and McCoy exchanged glances. "Why would he tell you to do that?"

Salazar looked him in the eye. "Because he iced her and didn't want her found."

"What did you do with her?"

"Took her to the Everglades, to Hell's Bay. You know, where the sharks and 'gators hang out."

Nick suddenly felt queasy. "Why did he kill her?"

"He said she was rippin' him off. She had some local bigshot on the hook, and she wasn't givin' Turk his cut. He did it to keep his other girls in line."

Nick leaned against the wall, crossing his arms over his chest. "That young woman had a family, and they've gone ten years not knowing what happened to her. Did you ever think about that?"

"Yeah, I thought about it, but I couldn't disobey Turk's orders."

"You just do whatever he tells you to do, don't you? Get rid of bodies, break people's legs, arrange gang rapes. It's all in a day's work for you, isn't it?"

Salazar looked him in the eye. "Look, man, I ain't proud of some of the shit I did, but I told you why I had to do it. Once you're in his pocket, you don't walk away, not if you wanna keep breathin'"

Nick motioned for McCoy to follow him across the room. "Don't go away," he told Salazar.

"No body, no case," Bones said. "Looks like we hit a dead end."

"Yeah. Salazar's testimony wouldn't be worth shit to the cops. With his record, Turk could just point the finger at Salazar and claim he killed the girl."

"If you wanna pin the murder on him, it looks like Jimmie Rae is our only bet."

"I don't want to put him through that if we don't need to.

If it went to trial, a defense attorney would chew him up on the witness stand for not reporting the murder ten years ago, and they'd bring up his drug habit. He wouldn't make a credible witness."

"How do we put him down for the count?"

Nick thought for a few moments. "Pin something on him that he can't buy his way out of."

McCoy took his cell phone from his pocket. "I almost forgot. I had someone monitor that mic you planted in Bahama Joe's and they got somethin'."

"What did they hear?"

"A phone conversation between Turk and his accountant from a coupla days ago. They sent me the audio file. Listen to this."

Turk demanded in an angry tone, "You're telling me that nearly a half-million dollars of my money vanished under your nose, and you have no idea where it is? . . . I don't care what safeguards you've put in place. I'm paying you to make certain things like this don't happen in the first place . . . Then I'll tell you what you're going to do. You're going to go over every account, every ledger, every transaction until you find out where that money went and who was responsible for stealing from me. If you can't come up with a logical answer, I'd suggest you move to a different country, one where I won't be able to find you. Is that clear?"

The call was disconnected. McCoy stopped the playback.

"Strike three," Nick said. "Anything since then?"

McCoy scowled. "No. It seems that someone set a fire and melted the mic."

Nick shrugged. "Sorry about that. Will you be okay babysitting Salazar?"

"Yeah. Where you goin'?"

"Home. I want to check in on Felicia and the girl and find out what she knows about Turk's operation."

McCoy handed him the car keys. "Don't stay out too late. I worry about you."

"Thanks, Dad. I promise to have the car back by midnight."

CHAPTER EIGHTEEN

Darkness had enveloped the Keys, accompanied by the familiar sounds of music and laughter drifting in from nearby restaurants and bars. Nick parked a few spaces down from his home to wait. He watched the parking lot entrance but didn't see any cars entering or driving by. When he was satisfied that he hadn't been followed, he went inside. The living room lights were low, and voices came from out back, along with soft music from the stereo. He went to the deck where Felicia and Jalisa sipped glasses of wine while talking. A small oil lamp in the center of the table produced a light that flickered with the gentle evening breeze.

"I'm sorry to crash your slumber party," he said.

Felicia sprang to her feet, then gave him a firm hug and a kiss. "Hey, tough guy. You should've called."

"You know how I like to surprise you."

"You haven't been formally introduced. Jalisa, this is Nick, the guy I was tellin' you about."

Jalisa smiled and extended her hand. "Nice to meet you."

He shook her hand. "The pleasure's mine. I hope you're comfortable here."

"Yes, thank you. You have a lovely home."

"Would you excuse us for a few minutes?"

He led Felicia inside and kissed her again.

"What was that for?" she asked.

"Because I've missed you. Got a problem with that?"

"Of course not."

He poured himself a tumbler of scotch on the rocks and

took a sip. "Any chance you were followed?"

Felicia shook her head. "I had a livery service take us to Florida City and called an Uber from there to bring us the rest of the way. I used a different pick-up spot than where we were dropped off, and I was watchin' the rearview all the way down. No one followed us."

He raised his glass. "Good work. How's Jalisa doing?"

"Not bad, but she's askin' a lot of questions."

"About what?"

"About what we're really doin' and why are we doin' it. I've put her off for now, but I don't know how much longer she'll buy it. She's a smart girl, and she knows something's up. Anything happen after last night?"

"No. We paid a surprise visit to Turk this afternoon a few hours before our planned meeting and caught him off guard."

"How did it go?"

"He wants to kill me."

"That means you're doin' your job. Where's Salazar?"

"Bones found a safe house in Homestead. He's there with him now."

"Anythin' come from what Jimmie told you?"

"Nothing we can use. Salazar admitted that he disposed of the girl's body on Turk's orders but without physical evidence, the police won't be able to do anything. I just feel bad for the girl's family. Did Jalisa shed any light?"

"A couple of things. Turk lures those young women with the promise of a show biz career, then uses them as B-girls and escorts for his friends."

He sipped his drink. "What's your read on her?"

"She has a lot of self-esteem issues, really down on herself. She doesn't think she's worth anyone's time or trouble. I had a hard time convincin' her that we were helpin' her because we wanted to and not because we expected somethin'."

"Do you think she wants to go back to Turk?"

Felicia shook her head. "She wants him to pay for what he did. When you talked with Jimmie, did you tell him what happened?"

"No. That's between them. If she wants him to know, she'll do it in her own time. Do you think she'll open up to me if I talk to her?"

"I think so. She's curious about you."

Nick's eyebrows arched. "Curious how?"

"She heard Turk talkin' about you bein' an international smuggler, and she wants to know if you're as crooked as he let on."

"Then let's satisfy her curiosity."

They went to the deck and took seats. Nick fired up a cigarette and asked, "Jalisa, do you get to The Keys very often?"

"Been to Key West once," she answered. "Don't really get out of Miami that much. I'm usually too busy workin'."

Nick nodded. "Yeah, I get that."

She took a drink of wine. "Felicia says you wanna cut Turk down to size."

"That's right."

"Why?"

Nick took a puff. "Why not?"

Jalisa looked him in the eye. "How can I help?"

He sipped his drink. "Tell me how he manages to get so many politicians and cops in his pocket."

Jalisa looked into her glass for a few moments. "You know he expects the girls at his place to play nice with his buddies, right?"

"Yeah, I heard that."

"When some of them want to get frisky, he has a private bedroom upstairs. What they don't know is that Turk has a video camera hidden in there."

Nick and Felicia looked at each other.

"That explains it," Felicia said.

"Is that how you do things in the places you run?" Jalisa asked.

Nick took a final puff, then extinguished his cigarette.

"Ya know, you really should quit those things," Jalisa said. "They're bad for you."

Nick looked at her. "Did Felicia tell you to say that?"

"We talked. She worries about you, but I'm not really sure why."

"Sounds like you talked a lot. Why don't you tell me what you've heard about me?"

"I heard that you're some kinda smuggler who works in Europe. You've got the reputation of bein' a real badass. Turk says you're tryin' to steal his people so they can work in your nightclubs and smuggle things in and out of the country."

"He personally told you all of that?"

"Not directly, but I heard about it."

"You'd like to know if it's true?"

Jalisa looked at him while a smile played across her lips. "Yeah. I'd like to know if I'm dealin' with an honest to goodness gangsta instead of some cheap wannabe."

Nick fought the laughter that threatened to burst forth. *Why not play along?* "Part of what he said is true."

"Which part?"

"The part about me being a badass."

"What about the rest of it?"

"Let's just say I've been around."

She sipped her drink. "What else do you wanna know?"

"Why don't you just talk."

"About what?"

"Anything you observed when you were in Turk's place, whether you think it's important or not. Just talk to us."

"I don't know where to start."

"Start with how you got involved with him."

She cradled her glass and stared into it. "I was singin' back-up for a guy on the Beach, me and two other girls. One night, Turk showed up in the audience. He came backstage after our set and told me I could do better if I came to work for him."

"That was all it took?"

Jalisa nodded. "That and more money than I was makin'. He never did give me a break, though. He had me work as a back-up singer for a couple of his other acts, but every time I asked about goin' solo, he gave me another piece of jewelry and put me off. Kept sayin' *When I think you're ready.*" She shook her head. "Can't believe how dumb I was."

"I'm curious. Did he ever give any of the other girls their big break?"

Jalisa looked at him. "The ones who slept with his buddies. That's prob'ly why he held me back."

"Did he know that you and Jimmie Rae were involved when he took you in?"

"It was known."

Nick sipped his drink as an idea came to him. "Did Turk ever get personally involved with any of the girls he kept around the bar?"

She took a drink. "He didn't have any one regular girl, just a lotta hit and miss. You know, sometimes he'd pick one to party with but drop her the next day, but a week later, there she was, back with him."

"They still came back for more?" Felicia asked.

"Most of 'em did."

"Sounds like you weren't so dumb, after all," Felicia said.

Jalisa gave a shy smile. "Thanks."

"Tell me about this dream project of his, that Funk music museum," Nick said.

"What about it?"

"He's been promising to build it for three years but hasn't yet. Is he really serious about it, or is he just using it to raise money and line his pockets?"

"I'm not sure. He doesn't talk business when any of the posse is around. He keeps a tight face about that kinda stuff." She drained her glass, then set it on the table. "Now that you mention it, about a month ago, some guy came into the club. He and Turk had a really intense conversation. I could tell Turk was gettin' hot."

"Do you know who this guy is?"

"One of the other girls told me he's some politician from Hialeah named Suarez."

Nick and Felicia traded glances.

"That's where Turk promised to build his museum," Felicia commented. "Near the racetrack, as I recall."

"Yeah, that's right," Jalisa confirmed.

"Did you hear anything else about it?" Nick asked.

She shook her head. "Like I said, he doesn't talk business around any of us." She gave a smirk. "Big man, some kinda saint to the community. He expects ev'ryone to kiss his ass, but they'd stomp his ass if they knew the truth."

"That's what we're looking for," Nick said.

"Since you brought it up, can I ask you somethin' now?"

"What did I bring up?"

"The truth. Felicia said you two aren't tryin' to take over Turk's turf. You rescued me the other night, which I appreciate, but I don't understand why you're goin' after him."

Nick took a sip while flipping a mental coin. "You're entitled to a few answers. The truth is, my name isn't Nick Stavros. It's Nick Seven, and I used to work for the CIA."

Jalisa's eyes widened. "You were a spook?"

"So was I," Felicia added.

"Wow," she softly said. "That's better than bein' a gangsta, but why are you goin' after Turk? Is he some kinda terrorist?"

"He's just a pain in the ass," Nick replied. "I might as well tell you the rest of it. I own a club down here called Cricket's Bayside. Jimmie plays there a few times a month. He told us what Turk Morgan was doing, and we decided to help."

"Why?"

"I guess we were bored," Felicia said.

"The point is," Nick continued, "we were just going to get Turk to leave you two alone, but the more we dug into his operation, we realized we should do something about him because the cops won't. End of story."

Jalisa looked at Felicia. "Some BFF you turned out to be, holdin' out on me like that."

Nick threw Felicia a confused look. "BFF?"

"It's a girl thing," she said. "Sorta like what you have with Bones."

Nick nodded in understanding, then addressed Jalisa. "I have to ask that you not tell anyone what I just shared with you, at least until this is over. Can I trust you to do that?"

Jalisa's face took on a sly smile. "Yeah, I can do that." She giggled. "Can't believe I'm sittin' here with a coupla spooks. That's really cool."

Felicia lightly smacked Nick's arm. "Told you we were cool, but you didn't believe me."

Nick pulled to a stop in the driveway of the safe house and shut off the engine. He had taken advantage of being at home to grab a quick shower and a change of clothes, exchanging his dress shirt for a dark blue crewneck, while still wearing the black suit. He got out of the car but hesitated as he looked at the house, sensing that something was off. The front door was ajar, and he heard loud voices from inside. He quietly approached to peek in through the front window.

Bones stood with his hands elevated, facing Salazar, who was pointing a gun at him. Jack lay in a heap on the floor, not moving, a nasty-looking gash on his forehead and blood seeping from the wound.

Nick ran to the rear of the house and jimmied open the back door that led to the kitchen. He quietly entered but stopped when he neared the living room, listening to the loud conversation.

"I said give me the fuckin' cell phone," Salazar commanded. "Give it to me, or I'll shoot your ass!"

"Just who are you gonna call?" Bones asked. "You think Turk is gonna come ridin' to your rescue after you bailed on him? He's already replaced you with a new boy."

"I'm callin' a cab so I can get the hell outta here." He raised the weapon and took direct aim. "Hand it over!"

Nick looked around the kitchen, spotted a frying pan and picked it up. He flung it across the living room to clatter against the wall. Salazar whirled in the direction of the noise, firing a shot in reflex. Nick tackled him from behind, pinning him to the floor while he struggled. Bones quickly scooped up the gun and tossed Nick a pair of handcuffs. Bracing his knee in the small of Salazar's back, Nick held him still, cuffing his hands behind his back. He wrestled Salazar to his feet, then forced him onto the chair. Nick took the rope from the floor and wrapped it around Salazar's waist, binding him tightly. Salazar began a loud protest, but Nick stuffed his handkerchief into Salazar's mouth.

He faced McCoy. "What the hell happened?"

"Jack untied him so he could use the can. Salazar got the jump on him and grabbed his gun."

"Where were you?"

"I stepped outside to make a call."

Nick knelt next to Jack and examined the gash to his forehead while Bones brought a first aid kit from the bathroom. Nick cleansed and dressed Jack's wound, then he and Bones carried him to the couch.

Nick gestured at the first aid kit. "Give me one of those ammonia capsules."

Bones handed him one of the gauze-wrapped glass tubes. Nick snapped it open and waved it under Jack's nose. Jack inhaled the noxious fumes and took in a sharp breath. His eyes fluttered open.

"Jack, can you hear me?" Nick asked.

"Yeah," he weakly replied before his eyes shut again.

Nick held the capsule under his nose again to bring him around.

"Open your eyes." He held up three fingers. "How many fingers do you see?"

Jack's rapidly blinking eyes focused. "Three."

"Do you know where you are?"

"Safehouse," he mumbled. He exhaled, then fell asleep, his breathing settling into a steady drone.

Nick stood. "He doesn't need stitches, but he'll have one helluva headache when he wakes up. I hope you offer your guys combat pay."

"I'll make it up to him. What did you find out?"

"Jalisa told me how Turk runs his blackmail scheme. His girls use a bedroom above Bahama Joe's to entertain his friends, and he records the proceedings."

Bones chuckled. "Nobody figured it out before it was too late?"

"Apparently, their blood settled somewhere south of the border."

"No wonder his ass is covered a dozen different ways."

"What kind of feedback are we getting from that online smear campaign?"

Bones held out his phone. "See for yourself."

Nick scrolled through several pages of posts, noting some calling for the authorities to investigate Turk Morgan's charitable foundations. Several posts confirmed what Nick had learned from Jimmie Rae about Turk's *quid pro quo* version of offering a helping hand to those in need. Some other posts questioned his intentions to build the Funk music museum.

"What about the one you posted on the girl he killed? Any responses yet?"

McCoy switched to a different screen. Nick read a reply from someone claiming to be Lashonda James' brother, asking anyone with information to come forward so the family could get some closure.

He gave Bones the phone. "Looks like it's gaining momentum, but it won't be enough to put him out of business."

"Not by itself, but I heard his dream project for that Funk center lost a couple of major backers after we planted this stuff."

"And the walls came tumbling down. Did one of those backers happen to include a politician from Hialeah named Suarez?"

"That name came up. How did you know?"

"Jalisa mentioned him. She said he and Turk got into an argument at Bahama Joe's."

"How's she holdin' up?"

"Pretty good. She thinks I'm cool."

Bones laughed. "Say what? Why does she think that?"

"I told her who I really am and what I used to do for a living."

"She thinks that makes you cool?"

"She said it's cooler than me being a gangsta."

"Why did you spill the beans?"

"She was asking Felicia a lot of questions. After what she's been through, I thought she deserved some answers. She's also smart and eventually would've figured out that we aren't really criminal masterminds out to take over Turk's operation."

"Aren't you worried that she'll tip him off?"

Nick shook his head. "She's out for blood."

"Now we know how he gets his protection, but how can

we use it? None of those people are gonna come forward."

"We need to catch him in the act, doing something he can't deny."

"Won't be easy. Turk has too many people doin' his grunt work."

"I've been thinking about that woman he killed. If he has guys like Salazar on a leash, why did he do the job himself?"

Bones thought. "Maybe there was a personal angle."

"Or perhaps it made him mad enough to lose his temper. You've seen how tightly wound he is. He's already on the run, and if we can get him to lose control again, he might do something reckless."

"What would send him off the deep end?"

Nick glanced at Salazar. "Coming face to face with someone who betrayed him."

Bones lowered his voice. "Are you seriously thinkin' of usin' Salazar as bait?"

"Why not? Think about what's going through Turk's mind right now. Salazar went off the radar, Vargas is in custody, and his bookkeepers told him there's a shortage in his bank accounts. I keep showing up and spouting more info about his business than I have a right to know. He even mentioned that when I talked to him the other day. He has to be thinking that Salazar spilled his guts."

Bones was silent for a few moments. "It could work."

Felicia repositioned herself in the bed, unable to find a comfort zone. She glanced at the clock on the nightstand. *Three hours and I still can't fall asleep. Damn you, Nick. Just when I need a warm body to cuddle with, you go AWOL.* She pulled Nick's pillow over, rolled onto her side, and clutched the pillow firmly. She closed her eyes and inhaled his scent. *Not as good as havin' the real thing here.*

Her mind drifted to the fateful day a few years earlier when

Nick had proposed their current co-habitation arrangement. Felicia had never pursued any man as potential husband material, opting to settle for comfortable casual relationships. Call her rebellious, call her stubborn or independent, but she had learned early on to fend for herself. Like Nick, she had experienced one heartbreak that left her devastated to the point she refused to take that kind of risk with her emotions again.

He lost a wife to a terrorist in Scotland, and I lost my first soul mate to a suicide bomber in Iraq. Different war, same fallout.

Life with Nick in what he called his personal corner of paradise had proved idyllic, with enough surprises to keep it from teetering on the mundane. He possessed enough spontaneity and zest for life to satisfy her restless nature. Beneath the hard shell exterior he let the public see lurked a very sensual and sexual soul, one of the most adventurous lovers Felicia had ever encountered. She recalled their intense mating ritual in Miami a few nights earlier and felt a warm internal glow. Felicia emitted a sigh.

Damn, I wish he was here tonight!

She raised up to answer a light tapping on the door. "Yeah?"

Jalisa stepped into the room, wearing an oversized t-shirt that reached her thighs. "I couldn't sleep. Can I come in?"

"Sure."

She approached the bed, and Felicia threw back the sheet. Jalisa climbed in and nestled against the pillows.

"Why couldn't you sleep?" Felicia asked.

"Ev'rything we were talkin' about before. Guess it brought back too many bad memories. Couldn't stop thinkin' about stuff."

"Feel like talkin' about it?"

"Not really. I just didn't want to be alone tonight."

Felicia sighed. "I hear you."

"You're really missin' your man, aren't you?"

"Is it that obvious?"

"I saw the way you two look at each other. You're really lucky, havin' a hot guy like him lookin' at you the way he did tonight."

Felicia grinned. "Yeah, Nick's a special guy. Jimmie is, too, the way he worries about you."

"You don't need to sell me 'cause I already made up my mind. When this is over, I'm gonna beg him to take me back."

"You won't have to beg much."

Felicia's eyes widened when Jalisa snuggled against her and rested her hand across her stomach. Her pulse quickened when Jalisa's hand traveled upward, stopping at her breast. "Hey, what're you doin'?" she asked.

"I just wanna pay you back for all the good you've been showin' me."

Felicia sat upright and faced her, the sheet sliding over her naked torso. "Jalisa, you don't have to say thanks like that."

Jalisa ran her fingers over Felicia's cheek. "What's wrong, baby? I just wanna make you feel good. I like a little girl time once in a while."

Felicia gently pulled Jalisa's hand away. "I don't really get into that."

"I'm sorry. Does that mean I have to leave?"

"No, you can stay but no foolin' around. Okay?"

"Okay. Sorry if I came on too strong."

"Forget about it. Just get some sleep."

Felicia slid back down into the bed and pulled the sheet over her. *Guess I overplayed the best friend thing.* She closed her eyes, but something from the nether regions of her memory nagged at her, something from the long ago and far away. *Why was I so harsh with Jalisa just now? Here I've been tryin' to forge a friendship with her the past few days, gain her trust, and I overreact when she makes a move. I shouldn't have done that.*

She looked over her shoulder. Jalisa was on her side, facing away from her. Felicia placed her hand on Jalisa's shoulder.

"Jalisa, are you awake?"

"No."

"Come on, girlfriend. Talk to me."

Jalisa rolled over to face her. "What do you wanna talk about?"

"I'm sorry I reacted the way I did. You just took me by surprise." She propped herself up on her elbow. "Do you know anythin' about Barbados?"

Jalisa shook her head. "Just that it's a long way from here."

"You know how we get tropical storms and hurricanes here?"

"Uh-huh. I hate it when the big blows come in and they make us evacuate."

"At least you have someplace to evacuate to. Try gettin' ready for one of those big blows when you're on a little island in the ocean a few hundred miles from anywhere else."

"Never thought about that. What do you do?"

"People there have been goin' through storms since who knows when, and they know how to get ready for one." She took a strand of Jalisa's hair between her fingers. "I told you I was the oldest in my family. When I was growin' up and a tropical storm would hit, where do you think my little sisters and brothers would run to when all hell was breakin' loose?"

Jalisa paused. "Your room?"

"You got it. They wanted big sis to keep them safe, to make them feel secure until it blew over. Durin' the hurricane season, I can't tell you how many night's sleep I lost because they all wanted to crowd in with me when my mom and dad's bed was filled."

"How many kids were in your family?"

"Eight."

"Damn! No wonder you had an active childhood. So, you're sayin' it's okay to cuddle during bad times?"

"I'm sayin' it's okay to be scared or lonely. We all need

someone to make us feel secure sometimes." She paused. "For what it's worth, I had some girl time once when I was younger, and I didn't care for it. I guess that's why I reacted the way I did. Sorry."

Jalisa glanced down. "No, I'm sorry. I don't do that very often, but I just wanted to pay you back for everything you've done for me." She raised her gaze. "Still friends?"

Felicia smiled. "Still BFF's. Goodnight."

CHAPTER NINETEEN

Nick called Felicia the following morning, just after daybreak. He stood outside the house in Homestead, watching the rising sun illuminate the tropical landscape. He stretched to loosen his back and leg muscles. It had been a restless night spent on the floor in one of the bedrooms. He and Bones had taken shifts guarding Salazar while Jack occupied the couch, sleeping off his bump on the noggin. Fortunately, he didn't appear to have a concussion or any other issues requiring emergency medical treatment.

"Good morning, angel. Sorry to roust you so early."

Felicia yawned. "That's okay. I couldn't sleep very well anyway."

"Why not?"

"You weren't here."

Nick chuckled. "That's the nicest thing I've heard in days."

"What's up?"

"I'm going to force Turk's hand so we can get this over with. I need you to run all those GPS locations on his car and establish a pattern."

"What are you lookin' for?"

"When he leaves his house, where he goes during the day, and when he comes home to roost. What I really need to know is if there's a place he goes on a regular basis at a regular time, someplace where we can confront him."

"Okay." She paused. "I really miss you, tough guy."

Nick felt a longing deep inside, one that wasn't sated by his visit the evening before. "I miss you, too. This will be over soon."

"Do you promise?"

"Have I ever lied to you?"

He went into the house and found McCoy, stripped to the waist, doing push-ups and breathing heavily. "What is this all about?"

McCoy got to his feet, then mopped his sweaty brow and head with a towel.

"You drink coffee, I work out. It braces me for the day. What's on the agenda?"

"Felicia's putting together a pattern of Turk's movements from his GPS. She'll send it to me."

McCoy draped the towel around his neck. "I've been thinkin' about that plan of yours. We should find a place where Turk feels safe, someplace he's kept hidden from ev'ry-one else."

"I agree. That's why I asked Felicia to put together a list. He has to have a comfort zone."

"I'm still not sure you tellin' the girl the whole story last night was a good idea. She might change her mind about blowin' the whistle on us."

"It was a gamble I had to take. I needed to gain her confidence, so she'd open up to me."

McCoy grabbed his shirt from the floor. "I'm gonna hit the shower. Take over for me?"

"Go for it."

Nick glanced at Salazar, still out of it with his chin resting on his chest. Jack was beginning to come back to life, mumbling incoherently in his sleep. Nick walked to the door and dialed Jimmie Rae's number.

"Jimmie, it's Nick. Are you all right?"

"Yeah, I'm okay. I'm stayin' with . . ."

"Don't tell me where you are. Have you seen any of Turk's people hanging around?"

"No. How's Jalisa?"

"She's okay."

"Can I talk to her?"

"Not yet. I know you're worried, but we're close to wrapping this up, and the less you know, the better. You just have to trust me, pal."

There was a pause. "Okay. What can I do?"

"Keep your head down and stay out of sight. If you see or hear anything odd, call me. I'll be in touch."

McCoy entered the room with a towel draped around his neck, wearing a long-sleeved black t-shirt and dark slacks.

"I just got a call from the guy I left at the condo on Miami Beach. One of Turk's men paid a visit, askin' the building manager if he'd seen you, Salazar, or the girl in the past coupla days. They sweated him and found out that Turk put tenthousand bucks on the streets for any info that leads to you."

Nick smirked. "Man, he really is a cheap hood. Anyone else would've put up twenty-five."

"He's got a bounty on us, man. With his network, we'll have to move very carefully."

"Sounds like we've got him on the run if he's putting out reward money. This could be the time to strike."

"That's what I'm thinkin', too."

Nick's cell phone chimed with an e-mail message from Felicia. The attachment contained a spreadsheet with the information he had asked her to compile. He read it, noting an address he hadn't seen before. He accessed the online map and typed in the address. When the result appeared, he showed it to McCoy.

"We have a winner," Nick said. "This address is in a residential neighborhood in Kendall. That's a long way from Boca Raton. Turk paid a visit there last Thursday, from ten to eleven-thirty."

"Could be business."

"I don't think so. Every other place we tracked him was one of his clubs or an office building somewhere."

"You thinkin' girlfriend?"

"I doubt he's visiting his mother. Can you run the address and get us the name of who lives there?"

"Done. Ya know, today's Thursday. If he keeps his regular routine, he'll be there tonight."

"Yeah. Think we can get something set up by then?"

McCoy chuckled. "Wouldn't be surprised."

Jimmie Rae walked along the sidewalk in Little Havana, his gaze darting from left to right, watching for anyone focusing their attention on him. All around him, emigres sidled up to pick-up windows and pushcarts to get cups of strong Cuban brew and native pastries, while tourists visited some of the shops in search of items supposedly imported from the forbidden land ninety miles away. Jimmie hadn't slept much the past few nights, the pressure of his current situation catching up with him. He took a deep breath and held it for a few beats before slowly exhaling.

Man, I hope Nick gets this mess settled pretty quick. Don't know how much more of this I can take.

He stepped into a bodega to purchase a breakfast burrito and coffee. Standing in front of the shop, eating, his thoughts drifted to Jalisa. The ache of longing in his gut intensified the more he visualized her. All of the good times they had shared came flooding back.

Nick said she was safe, and she was okay, but I need to see that for myself. Why wouldn't he tell me where she is? Was he afraid I'd show up and spoil things? He could at least let me talk to her.

Jimmie replayed the conversations he and Nick had earlier and realized this situation was more serious than he originally thought. Turk Morgan wasn't one to go away quietly or with empty hands, a fact Jimmie knew all too well. He had seen firsthand how the man operated, how he used and manipulated others to get what he wanted. Jimmie also knew if the other person had nothing to give, Turk would settle for blood, one drop at a time.

He finished his burrito. Tossing the wrapper to a nearby trash can, something caught his eye from across the street. He looked in that direction. A tall, thin black man wearing a purple running suit eyed Jimmie.

Damn! I know that dude. He's part of Turk's street crew from Overtown.

Jimmie walked back the way he'd come at a rapid clip. He glanced over his shoulder. The other man crossed the street, following him. Jimmie dodged other people on the street while looking for a place to hide.

"Yo, Jimmie Rae," the other man called out. "Wait up, man."

Knowing it was pointless to try to avoid a confrontation, Jimmie stopped.

The man caught up with him. "Thought that was you," he said. "What you up to these days?"

Jimmie put on the most relaxed air he could muster. "Just workin', man. You know how it is."

The man nodded. "You still got that little girl you were hangin' with? What was her name—Jalisa?"

"Nah, we broke up. She moved out on me."

"Too bad. Where's she keepin' herself these days?"

Jimmie's pulse quickened. He shrugged. "Don't know, man. She didn't leave a forwarding address." He glanced at his watch. "Hate to cut this short, but I got people to see."

"Sure, man." He took a card from his pocket and handed it over. "That's my cell. Since that girl ain't with you no more, I wouldn't mind a hook-up if it's okay with you. You find out where she is, holler at me."

Jimmie pocketed the card. "On the real, man. See ya."

He continued on his way. After turning the next corner, he stopped. He peeked around the building but didn't see anyone following him. Jimmie took out his cell phone and tapped Nick's number. After four rings it went to voicemail. "Nick, this is Jimmie. I just ran into one of Turk's guys on the street. He was askin' about Jalisa, wanted to know how he could get hold of her. Just thought you ought to know."

He pocketed the phone, then let out a deep breath. *Guess I need to find someplace new to hide until this blows over.*

"I got the four-one-one on that address in Kendall," McCoy said. "The resident is one Jacqueline Cooper."

"Anything noteworthy about her?" Nick asked.

McCoy looked at his phone screen. "Used to be a singer in a girl group called the South Beach Divas. Gave that up last year when they disbanded."

Nick sipped his coffee. "Another music and nightclub connection. Turk probably handled the act. How long has she lived at that address?"

"A year, but there's more. The house is actually owned by one of Turk's charities. It's registered as a safe house for battered women, and she's listed as the home manager. She even receives state and local funding for household expenses and utilities."

"Man, I love it when they get careless. I'm guessing if we visit, we won't find any domestic violence victims staying there."

"I'd take that bet. We found somethin' else. I had one of my analysts look at all those credit card charges I sent you. The florist where he places a weekly order delivers to that address every Thursday. They also checked the calendar on Salazar's phone, and it's listed as a standing appointment over the last six months."

"Looks like we've got him."

"You still wanna have a showdown there?"

"Yeah. His guard will be down since he's likely visiting his girlfriend. Did you cut back on Salazar's drug cocktail?"

"I gave him enough to make him sleep, but he'll just be groggy by the time we move out."

"Good. For this to work, we need him to be semi-coherent."

"I still think this plan of yours could use some fine-tuning."

"If you have a better idea, lay it on me."

McCoy shook his head. "I'm fresh out."

Nick's cell phone chimed, letting him know he had a new voicemail. He listened to it, hearing Jimmie Rae's message.

"Damn!"

"What's wrong?"

"That was Jimmie Rae. One of Turk's men saw him on the street and talked to him. Jimmie said this guy was asking about Jalisa and if Jimmie knew how to get in touch with her."

"Good thing you didn't tell him where she is. What if he tries callin' her?"

"Felicia took her phone into protective custody." He looked at his watch. "We can't move out until later today, and if Turk has people looking for us, we need to stay off the radar. Any suggestions on how to pass the time?"

"Give me a chance to win back what I lost to you in poker the other day."

"You're being awfully generous with Salazar's money."

CHAPTER TWENTY

Felicia washed the breakfast dishes in the kitchen sink. She'd prepared an eye-opener of eggs and focaccia toast with coffee and orange juice. After eating, Jalisa had retreated to the shower. Felicia wasn't sure how to react to her after the unwanted overture she had made the night before.

How am I supposed to act, since she came on to me? Do I blow it off like nothin' happened? Do I say somethin'? More to the point, did I give her the idea that I wanted her to make a move?

Jalisa entered the kitchen. "Hey, what're you doin'? I said I'd clean up."

"It'll just take me a few minutes."

Jalisa sat on one of the bar stools at the counter. "Are you upset with me about last night?"

Felicia dried her hands on a towel, facing her. "No, not really. You just took me by surprise, that's all."

Jalisa cast her gaze on the counter. "I'm sorry."

Felicia had a nagging feeling, one that had to be satisfied. "Jalisa, did I give off a vibe that I wanted you to do that?"

She shook her head. "Not really."

"Then why did you do it?"

Jalisa looked at her. "Because you're the first person in a long time who really gave a damn about me." She shrugged. "Maybe I just, you know, felt close to you."

Felicia took a moment to process what Jalisa said. Over the past couple of days, she'd found herself thinking about the family she left behind on Barbados. A lifetime of memories

179

came flooding back, things from her childhood and adolescence she hadn't thought about for a long time. *Did I form an attachment to Jalisa because I've missed playin' big sister to my siblings?*

She freshened her coffee, then took a sip. "Jalisa, I've been thinkin' about what you said the other day, about growin' up in Liberty City."

"What about it?"

"You said you didn't have a big sister to bounce things off of, but there must've been someone you could talk to, like a teacher or a friend from school."

She was silent for a few moments. "Not really. Why are you askin'?"

"I'm tryin' to figure out where this low self-esteem stuff came from."

Jalisa stared at the counter. "I was pretty much on my own since I was twelve. Always had to hustle for things." She slowly shook her head. "Seemed like I always gettin' into fights with someone from the 'hood over somethin' stupid, like a pair of shoes somebody threw out that were better than the ones I had. Always stuff like that."

"I can't really relate to that."

Jalisa gave a small smile. "That's okay. I wouldn't wish it on anyone." She hesitated. "Since we're talkin', can I ask you somethin'?"

"Of course."

"You know I want to get back with Jimmie when this is over, but maybe I'm afraid I'll screw it up again." Jalisa looked at her. "You seem to have it together with this Nick guy. What should I do to make things work this time?"

Felicia drank some coffee while thinking of a good response. She wasn't sure if she had one. She'd never really thought about it. She knew that relationships were like walking a tightrope over a shark tank. Watch your footing, don't lose sight of your objective, stay alert, and whatever you do, don't let your mind or eyes wander, or you might lose your balance. Then a splash, a lot of thrashing, and it was over.

She placed her hand over Jalisa's. "This may disappoint you, but I don't really have a one-size-fits-all answer. We just clicked and found a lot of things we had in common. The longer we were together, the more things we discovered about each other. You and Jimmie must've shared some of those things."

Jalisa grinned shyly. "We did."

"Give me an example."

She giggled. "It's gonna sound silly."

"Try me."

"Some nights, when I was feelin' low, Jimmie would get out his guitar and sing to me. He'd make up words for songs he knew I liked, and they were all about me. Sometimes they were funny, and he'd get me to laugh. Always made me feel better."

Felicia laughed along with her. "That's sweet. Anything else?"

Jalisa appeared to be embarrassed. "Sometimes the lyrics he made up about us weren't the kind he could sing in public."

Felicia laughed a bit harder. "Now that's really sweet. Were you embarrassed when he did that?"

She shook her head. "I knew it was just for us, and nobody else would ever hear 'em. It made me feel closer to him."

Felicia squeezed her hand. "I don't think you'll have any problems."

McCoy slowed the car to a stop across the street from the house in Kendall. The neighborhood was quiet, no pedestrians were out walking their dogs, and the houses appeared to be in good repair. A streetlight near the house they were targeting emitted enough light to highlight the front area while providing adequate darkness to keep them in the shadows.

Nick studied the house, a typical southern Florida single-story dwelling, light stucco with an orange tiled roof and a front porch with two wicker chairs. Two hanging planters with ferns hung from the eaves, one on either side of the three concrete steps. The small front lawn was cut and dotted with hibiscus bushes. He scanned the surrounding area. He pointed at a darkened house across the street with a For Sale sign in the front yard.

"Looks like that's our vantage point. You have our escape route?"

"Uh-huh. After I drop you and Salazar off, I'll park on the next block. We'll haul ass between these houses."

Nick pressed a button on the side of his watch to illuminate the face. "Nine-thirty. Let's get in position."

McCoy coasted down the block to the empty house. He and Nick pulled Salazar from the back seat. His hands were cuffed behind his back and a strip of duct tape covered his mouth. He was unsteady so they helped him to the driveway next to the house and sat him down against the dwelling.

"Be back in a few," McCoy said.

While McCoy moved the car, Nick observed the house across the street.

Watching and waiting, just like the bad old days on stakeouts. This whole caper has served one good purpose. It's reminded me that any doubts I had about getting out of the spy game were proved wrong.

He took a pair of vinyl gloves from his coat pocket and slipped them on, then got Salazar's gun from his other pocket. He injected a bullet into the chamber. A few minutes later, McCoy joined him from behind.

"All set," he said in a low voice. "We run between these houses to the next street over. Should be a clean getaway."

Nick heard the sound of a vehicle approaching. Turk's car pulled into the driveway across the street.

"Right on time," he said.

Nick moved a few steps closer to the edge of the house, then knelt on one knee, pointing the gun as Turk and Rico exited the car and strolled to the porch steps. Nick took careful aim at the car, squeezing off two shots, splintering the rear window and one on the passenger side.

Turk and Rico whirled in the direction of the shots, and Rico pulled his gun from under his shirt. Nick fired another shot that shattered a ceramic planter hanging directly behind him, covering him with plaster fragments and potting soil. Both men momentarily froze. Nick's next two shots landed near Turk's feet, followed by another that barely missed his bulky frame, embedding itself in the stucco side of the house.

Rico ran to the front porch while Turk made a dash for the car. As he reached for the passenger door handle, Nick fired a shot that took out the side mirror inches from his arm. Flinging himself face first onto the ground, Turk cursed loudly. The next round landed near Turk's head. He scrambled to his feet, running to the porch for cover.

"Now," Nick said in a low tone.

McCoy pulled Salazar upright and removed the cuffs from his wrists. He ripped off the duct tape, shoving the Spaniard toward the street on rubbery legs. Nick pressed the gun into Salazar's hand as he passed. Salazar staggered to the curb, his gun-wielding hand hanging at his side. He came to a stop, his legs trembling, and his body swaying slightly.

Across the street stood Turk and Rico. Turk let out a loud yell that turned into a primal scream, grabbed Rico's gun, and aimed it at Salazar.

"Damn Judas!" he yelled, pulling the trigger.

Six shots found their way into Salazar's chest and belly. His hands flew into the air, and he danced backward before collapsing, the front of his shirt covered in blood. He exhaled a final deep breath, his body deflating.

The sound of approaching sirens filled the air. Turk and Rico looked in the direction of the noise. Nick took advantage of their distraction to scoop up Salazar's gun while McCoy picked up the spent brass shell casings. They ran to the back of the house, over to the one next door, scaled a chain link fence, and dodged some lawn furniture. They emerged from the side of the house and peered around the corner to watch the action. Porch lights lit up along the street as people ventured out to see what the commotion was.

Two police cruisers screeched to a stop and four uniformed officers bounded out, drawing their weapons. One of them took the gun from Turk's hand while another one patted down Rico.

Turk pointed across the street and told his story in his best fire and brimstone voice. "That man tried to kill me. He was lying in wait to assassinate me, just like they did to the good Dr. King. I fired in self-defense."

Two officers had gone to Salazar. One squatted to check for a pulse while the other one scanned the area with a flashlight.

"Hey, Sarge," he called out. "There's no weapon over here."

"I'm telling you that man was armed!" Turk screamed. "He came here to kill me!"

The first two officers placed handcuffs on Turk and Rico while one of the others radioed for back-up.

"You can't arrest me!" Turk proclaimed while being led to the cruiser. "Do you know who I am? I'm Turk Morgan! I will not be treated this way!"

He continued his rant while struggling with the officer fighting to get him into the car.

"I said I'm Turk *fucking* Morgan! This is a blatant violation of my civil rights and racial profiling by a corrupt police department! You can't do this to me!"

"Get in the car and shut up," the officer ordered. "Don't make me Tase you."

Nick and Bones continued watching as two more patrol cars and an emergency response team arrived. Rotating blue and red lights washed over the houses. The patrol officers began taking statements from the neighbors while the paramedics tended to Salazar. Two technicians cordoned off the area and began marking and photographing the scene. The whole thing was well choreographed, and everyone went through their paces like it was a macabre floor show, just another shooting on another dark street, like a thousand other nights in Magic City. No surprises, nothing to get excited about.

Nick stared at the police cruiser. He could still hear Turk's loud protests in spite of the door being shut. "Praise the Lord," he muttered.

"Huh?"

"Nothing. Let's get outta here."

They sprinted between the houses to the car one street over. Several minutes after they pulled away, Bones spoke. "You were right about Turk. You pushed his buttons, and he lost control. You think that's what happened when he killed that woman?"

"We'll never know, will we?"

Another silence followed before Bones spoke again. "You still got it, Nick."

Nick grinned. "Thanks. So do you." He paused for a few moments. "Since there was no payoff for you this time, if you want to claim the credit for taking Turk down, it's all yours. Just leave my name out of it."

Bones chuckled. "Thanks, but I'm not sure that's the kind of press I can use. Want me to take you home?"

Nick took out his cell phone. "After we make a stop."

Felicia and Jalisa sat on the deck, sipping wine and listening to music. The night was still, the clear evening sky dotted with stars. A light breeze blew in across the channel, making the windchimes play a carefree tune.

"Sure is nice out here," Jalisa commented. "I could get used to this."

"It can be habit-forming," Felicia said. She took a sip before continuing. "You given any thought to what you'll do now?"

Jalisa looked at her. "You mean now that I'm not in Turk's stable any longer? Try to get my life and career back on track." She hesitated. "Sure would be nicer if Jimmie was a part of it."

Felicia took her hand and squeezed it. "I have a feelin' that'll work out."

She was startled by a familiar voice behind her.

"Did you start the party without me?" Nick asked.

Felicia looked around in surprise and smiled. She scrambled to her feet and gave him a tight hug followed by a lingering kiss. "Hey, tough guy. I didn't know you were comin' home."

"You never know when I'll turn up." He looked at the table. "You'll need three more glasses."

"Three?"

"I brought company." He turned to the open patio door. "You can come out now."

Jimmie Rae emerged from the doorway, followed by McCoy. Jalisa gasped. She ran to Jimmie, throwing her arms around him.

He gave her a long kiss, pulled back, and placed his palm on her cheek. "Hey, baby."

"Hey yourself, Jimmie Bear." She paused. "Jimmie, I'm sorry for runnin' out on you like I did. I shouldn't have done that."

"No worries, Jalisa. We're back together now, and that's all that counts."

"You gonna let me stay around?"

"For as long as you can stand me."

Felicia put her arm around Nick's waist and leaned against him as they watched them kiss and make up

"Don't you love a happy ending?" she asked.

"Yeah, I do."

"Speakin' of which, is everything else okay now?"

"They won't have any more problems." He took Felicia's hand. "Let's give these two some privacy."

They joined McCoy in the kitchen. Nick took out a bottle of his best scotch along with three glasses. After adding ice cubes, he poured a healthy amount into each tumbler and handed them out. He raised his in a toast.

"To the end of a successful operation," he said.

They touched their glasses, then each took a sip.

"You gonna tell me what happened?" Felicia asked.

"I think it's safe to say that Turk Morgan has made his last hostile takeover," Nick said.

"He's down for the count?" Felicia asked.

McCoy chuckled. "Girl, he's so far down, even Lazarus couldn't resurrect him."

"You should've seen him tonight," Nick said. "Mister High and Mighty getting cuffed by the cops and throwing his name around at the top of his ever-loving voice. It was actually kinda pathetic."

"What about Salazar?" Felicia asked.

Nick shook his head. "He was collateral damage."

Felicia sipped her drink. "Maybe Jalisa got some payback, after all."

Nick walked into the bedroom and tossed his suit jacket on a chair, followed by his shoulder holster and gun. He kicked off his shoes, then collapsed on the bed, exhaling a deep breath. He closed his eyes. *Definitely glad this is over. I'm happy it turned out the way we planned, but I don't want to do this very often.*

Felicia curled up next to him, and her hand rested on his chest. He opened his eyes, rolled over, and kissed her. A soft lingering kiss reminded him how much he had missed her the past few days. He inhaled her sweet scent, the one that always got to him.

Felicia pulled back slightly, brushing her hand over his brow. "Welcome home."

"I'm happy to be here. Thanks for everything you did."

"You don't have to thank me. I wanted to help." She paused. "Tell you somethin'?"

"Sure."

Her fingers lightly traced his cheek and jaw. "I learned a few things from this. One is how maybe I take what we have for granted sometimes."

"Why do you think that?"

"Just listenin' to Jalisa talk about how much she missed Jimmie after she walked out on him, and she realized it was a mistake. She didn't think she could have a life with him and a career for herself. It made me think that if you work it right, you really can have it both ways."

Nick placed his hand on the back of her neck under her hair. "What else did you learn?"

"That I missed you more than I thought I would. I didn't like spendin' nights without you." She hesitated before asking, "Did you miss me like that?"

Nick kissed her. "Definitely. I learned something, too."

"What?"

"McCoy snores."

Felicia laughed. "I could've gone the rest of my life without knowin' that." She tugged at his shirt, pulling it from his waist. "Why are you still dressed if we're in bed together for the first time in days?"

They quickly undressed, tossed their clothes on the floor, and reclined on the bed. Nick pulled Felicia in close, giving her deep kisses while running his hands over her smooth skin. Her hands roamed his shoulders and back, pulling him closer. Nick's hard-on pressed against her as he devoured her mouth, the longing of the previous days increasing his arousal.

Felicia reached down to fondle and squeeze him. Nick's hand slid down her torso, coming to rest on her pubic patch while his middle fingers slipped between her legs, teasing her and getting her wet. Their kissing increased in intensity, their tongues dueling with each other.

She broke their kiss, moving down to Nick's groin to take him into her mouth. She sucked him slowly, lovingly, savoring him while moaning softly. She bobbed up and down, working more of his length into her mouth. Nick closed his eyes, lightheaded and giddy, something he had missed the past few days.

Felicia stopped her oral stimulation to mount him, one knee on either side of his thighs. She grasped his cock, eased it between her legs, taking in a short gasp as she worked his length into her wet tunnel. She leaned forward, rested her open palms on his chest, rocked up and down, slowly, agonizingly until he was fully embedded inside her.

"I missed you," she whispered while moving against him.

Nick put his hands on her firm breasts, tweaking her nipples until they were like two gumdrops. "I missed you, too."

His hands went to Felicia's ass to rub and squeeze her cheeks. She lay across his torso and kissed him while continuing to move against him, getting wetter the longer they made love. His hands squeezed her ass, and her breasts rubbed against his chest, increasing his arousal.

Felicia sat upright, put her hands on his chest and moved faster, tightening around him as his shaft rubbed against her clit.

"Oh, hon," she moaned. "I'm coming!"

She moved faster when her climax hit, her pussy tightening around him with each spasm. Nick swelled and exploded inside her, his longing of the past few days finally quenched. They remained locked as one after their orgasms subsided, reveling in the afterglow of satisfying sex. Felicia raked her long fingernails over Nick's flesh while he rubbed her ass and thighs.

She collapsed on top of him, and they exchanged deep, wet kisses.

"This is what I really missed," Felicia whispered.

"Me, too. I don't ever want us to be apart like that again."

She kissed him. "Sleepin' without you next to me was almost impossible."

He caressed her cheek. "I had the same problem, but daybreak was when I felt it the worst."

"Why?"

"Because it reminded me how much I look forward to starting each day with you. It just wasn't the same."

Felicia raised up slightly, running her fingers over his sweaty brow. "Still partners in the game of life?"

Nick reached up and lightly fingered the angel pendant dangling from her neck. "Right up to the finish line."

Nick and Felicia sat at their usual table on Cricket's deck a few nights later. Jimmie Rae was back on stage, but with Jalisa as part of the act. They had worked up some duets along with her solo pieces, and the crowd seemed to appreciate the change.

"I'm still not paying him enough," Nick said. "We should

do something about that."

"That would be a nice thing to do, considerin' what they've been through," Felicia said. "Did you read the Miami newspaper this morning?"

"Just the comics and my horoscope. Did I miss something?"

"They had a follow-up on Turk Morgan's arrest. The Feds are lookin' into his charities to see what he's been hidin', and the cops released their initial report about the shooting. Seems they didn't find a gun anywhere near Salazar's body, even though Turk's still claimin' self-defense. They found a lot of bullets but there was no gunshot residue on Salazar's hands or clothes. Real mystery."

Nick gazed into the Gulf. "Is there a point to this?"

"I'm just curious since you skimmed over some of the details about what went down that night. Will they ever find that gun?"

Nick hesitated for a few moments. "Only if they go scuba diving in Biscayne Bay."

Felicia laughed softly. "That's my tough guy, always one step ahead."

When the set was over, Jimmie and Jalisa made their way through the crowd of well-wishers and selfie-takers to Nick's table.

"Great set, man," Nick said. "Jalisa, I didn't know you had such a pretty voice. You two really blend well."

She glanced down and gave an embarrassed grin. "Thank you, Mr. Nick."

Nick's eyebrows arched. "Mister? When did we get so formal?"

Jalisa shrugged. "It's the polite thing to do since I'm workin' for you. I'm surprised that someone as smart as you didn't know that."

Felicia chuckled. "I told you she was tough."

"Yeah, you warned me."

"Nick, can I ask a favor?" Jimmie asked.

Nick groaned and rolled his eyes. "Another mobster with his hooks in you?"

Jimmie laughed. "Nothin' quite so sinister." He glanced at Jalisa for a moment. "Jalisa and I are gettin' married, and we'd like you and Felicia to stand up for us, if you would."

Nick and Felicia exchanged surprised looks.

"We'd be honored and congratulations," Nick said.

Felicia squeezed Jalisa's hand. "Way to go, girlfriend."

"Thank you," she said as she gave Jimmie a dreamy-eyed gaze. "Maybe we can keep each other out of trouble."

Jimmie peered into her eyes. "When I audition for that record producer next month, Jalisa's gonna be part of the act, because we're a team now."

Nick raised his drink in a toast. "Wise decision. When you make the big time, you're still gonna play for us, though, right?"

Jimmie laughed. "Of course. After what you did for us, I owe you."

"We were glad to do it."

They went back for their next set and launched into *Never Gonna Let You Go*. The looks they exchanged gave more depth to the lyrics. It wasn't just two singers clicking together for the benefit of a song but the true passing of emotions between two people in love. Nick grinned when they reached the verse and he caught Jalisa flashing a quick wink and smile at Jimmie when she emphasized the word *never*. He thought he heard her say *Jimmie Bear* but he couldn't be sure.

"They make a nice lookin' couple," Felicia commented. "He's a lucky guy."

Nick looked into her eyes. "He isn't the only lucky guy in the place tonight."

Felicia cast her eyes down in embarrassment and absently

brushed a strand of hair back from her face. "I feel pretty lucky, too. You think we should follow their example?"

Nick's eyes widened slightly. "You mean getting married?"

"No, not gettin' married. We already decided that's a bad idea. I meant the part about keepin' each other out of trouble."

"I don't know. That could be a full-time job."

"I can handle it."

Nick gave her a blank look. "I was talking about me."

She laughed. "You sayin' I need you to keep me out of trouble?"

He shrugged. "Sometimes, you can be a little reckless."

"Name one time," she challenged.

"Like when you let that pizza delivery guy into the condo. You could've handled that better."

"At least I didn't set fire to a South Beach nightclub. That was what I'd call reckless."

"Yeah, I suppose it was." He peered into her soft, doe-like brown eyes. "Maybe I do need you to keep me on the right path."

She leaned over and kissed him, letting her lips linger near his. "Glad we settled that, partner."

The End

YOU MAY ALSO ENJOY THE FOLLOWING FROM EXTASY BOOKS INC:

Once Upon a Sunset
Tim Smith

Excerpt

Ted Allen walked into Ballyhoo's Historic Seafood Grill and looked around. The old-style décor hadn't changed in the five years since he'd last visited. He inhaled, and the welcome aromas of fresh seafood and steaks being grilled brought back a flood of memories. He sat at the bar and smiled as he looked at the framed black-and-white fishing photos and old advertising signs adorning the walls. They coordinated nicely with the 1930s-style walnut bar and matching barstools, evoking the Florida Keys of old, where fishermen and charter boat skippers hung out drinking shots and swapping tall tales about the ones that got away.

The bartender approached and slowly wagged his finger at him. "I know you. Scotch and soda with a lime twist. Right?"

Ted laughed. "Helluva way to be remembered, but you're right. How you been, Andy?"

"Good. Whatever happened to you?"

"I took a job in Nashville five years ago and had to move."

Andy nodded. "Now I remember. Your friends threw you

a going away party in here. I made a killing that night."

"Guilty as charged." He looked around. "Glad to see the place hasn't changed. This was always my favorite hang-out." He hesitated. "Does Shakira still work here?"

"Worse than that. She got promoted to manager."

"No shit. When does she work?"

Andy glanced at the wall clock. "Should be here any time." He fixed Ted's drink, then set it in front of him. "I'll send her over."

Ted sipped his drink and recalled things from the long-ago past. Shakira was one of the hottest women I've ever been with. Slight Jamaican-American accent, killer body and the sex drive of a nymphomaniac. Her skin was always soft and smelled of shea butter. He grinned. And those soft brown eyes you could lose yourself in. They were crazy eyes. All the times we made love, I always sensed there was something dark lurking beneath the surface, communicated by those eyes. I wonder if she's seeing anyone? Will she want to see me? It's been five years, and we haven't talked or written in nearly two. Maybe she's moved on.

He looked at his reflection in the mirror behind the bar. His light brown hair was windblown and his lean face had picked up some sun since he had arrived the day before. He squinted, his blue eyes no longer accustomed to the Florida sun. He recalled other things about his relationship with Shakira. Before I left, we were actually talking about making it a permanent thing. Then my job transferred me and we lost touch. Probably should've taken the plunge when I had the opportunity.

He shifted his gaze toward the cash register and his breath caught when he saw Shakira looking over the receipts. She hadn't changed since he last saw her, still trim, with a full bosom and tight ass that strained against her snug jeans. Her brown hair was a little longer than Ted remembered, cascading to her shoulders, but her bronzed skin was still smooth and her full lips were inviting. The five years of separation suddenly evaporated, replaced by a torrent of pleasant memories of the times they had spent together and all the fun things they had done. Definitely one of my bigger mistakes, not insisting that she come with me when I got that job offer up north.

Shakira turned in his direction but instantly stopped, her eyes widening when she saw him. She smiled warmly as she approached.

"Ted?" she asked, the smile growing.

"I know it's been awhile, but yeah, it's me. How are you, Shakira?"

She leaned over the bar with open arms and hugged him. Ted inhaled her scent, a pleasant mix of White Diamonds and her natural body chemistry.

"Are you here on vacation?" she asked.

"Better than that. I took a new job down here."

She leaned forward, resting her arms and full bosom on the bar.

Ted tried not to stare, but it wasn't easy.

"Doing what?"

"Guest services manager for one of the big hotel chains. They have five resorts in the Keys and Miami, and I get to ride roughshod over all of them."

"Congratulations. What happened with the job you had with that place in Nashville?"

"My contract was up so I decided to come back here." He let his eyes roam over her. "You look good, Shakira."

She glanced down shyly and smiled. "Thanks. So do you."

"So how are things? Andy said you were promoted to manager."

"Busy, but I'm doing okay." She paused. "So why haven't I heard from you lately?"

He took a sip before responding. "No excuses, but I'm sorry I didn't keep in touch. I really missed you."

She took his hand in hers and returned his dreamy gaze. "I missed you, too."

He laughed softly. "Now that we have the gee-you-look-great stuff out of the way, what else have you been up to?"

"If you're asking if I'm currently involved, the answer's no." She hesitated. "Are you?"

He shook his head. "Only with my work. I'm glad you're still here."

"That's me — just a homebody. Where are you staying?"

"I took a bungalow at the Coconut Bay Resort until I find something permanent." He paused again. "Want to stop over after you finish work tonight so we can catch up?"

Her eyebrows arched. "You don't waste time, do you?"

"Not with you. Shakira, I know it's been awhile and this might be out of line, but I never got over you."

She smiled shyly. "I never got over you, either. I'll admit I was upset when you stopped writing, but I figured you'd found someone else."

"No one that measured up to you."

She gave a soft, lyrical laugh. "We were pretty good together, weren't we?"

"So good that you spoiled me for other women."

She peered into his eyes. "I get off at eleven. What's your room number?"

About the Author

Tim Smith is an award-winning, bestselling author of romantic mystery/thrillers and contemporary erotic romance. He is also a freelance writer, blogger, and photographer. When not writing, he can often be found in The Florida Keys, doing research while indulging his passion for parasailing and seeking out the perfect Mojito.

www.ingramcontent.com/pod-product-compliance
Lightning Source LLC
Chambersburg PA
CBHW070845120626
46556CB00002B/887